ANNA SPARROWS

Anson's Awakening

Kinks & Conundrums Book 1

Contents

Preface	iii
Acknowledgments	iv
Chapter One – Anson	1
Chapter Two – Drake	5
Chapter Three – Anson	10
Chapter Four – Drake	16
Chapter Five – Anson	19
Chapter Six – Drake	30
Chapter Seven – Anson	33
Chapter Eight – Drake	39
Chapter Nine – Anson	45
Chapter Ten - Drake	52
Chapter Eleven – Anson	60
Chapter Twelve – Drake	67
Chapter Thirteen – Anson	80
Chapter Fourteen – Drake	86
Chapter Fifteen – Anson	94
Chapter Sixteen – Drake	105
Chapter Seventeen – Anson	115
Chapter Eighteen – Drake	123
Chapter Nineteen – Anson	127
Chapter Twenty – Drake	139
Chapter Twenty-One – Anson	148
Chapter Twenty-Two – Drake	157

Chapter Twenty-Three - Anson   168
Chapter Twenty-Four - Drake   178
Epilogue – Anson   181
DKAG Christmas Daddies   187
About the Author   189
Also by Anna Sparrows   191

Preface

Anson's Awakening is a super sweet, very low angst, *incredibly* fluffy Christmas age play novel featuring a first-time Little, a cinnamon roll Daddy, and a *lot* of sugar and steam. You *will* get cavities from this one.

CW: This novel contains ABDL and wetting, a *tiny* bit of hurt/comfort, some themes of self-doubt, and an itsy, bitsy hint of minor miscommunication (but absolutely no breakups or arguing. It's Christmas!)

Acknowledgments

Firstly, a massive thank you to A.W. Scott for inviting me to be a part of the DKAG Christmas Collaboration — even though this book functions as Book 1 of Kinks & Conundrums, it is starting its journey as part of the Daddy Kink & Age Gap Group Christmas collab for 2025. I'm still blown away that you asked me to join alongside all the other amazing Daddy kink authors. Thank you.

Off the back of that, Joe Satoria designed the cover for the DKAG Christmas release and it was gorgeous. Thank you so much for the work you do!

Speaking of covers, the Kinks & Conundrums cover was designed by the amazing Ky at Blue Brolli Graphics, and it is beyond perfect. Thank you!

Thank you to my wonderful alpha readers, Megan & Cindy, who helped take this from a collection of fluffy scenes, to something resembling very light plot. (It's a Christmas romance — I didn't want a lot of plot, haha.)

Similarly, thank you to Amanda, Erin, Myf & Fjord for beta reading. Your reader reactions helped settle my nerves, and to my PA, Ky, for dealing with my crazy ramblings as I tried to get the draft written.

Finally, thank you to you, the reader, for picking this book up. I warn you, it is cavity-inducingly sweet. Quite possibly the sweetest thing I've ever written. I hope you enjoy it!

Chapter One – Anson

This was a mistake.

The thought hits me as the snow dramatically shifts from whimsical flurries to ominous downfall. I've got my wipers going as fast as they can, and I'm gripping my steering wheel for dear life.

What the ever-loving fuck was I thinking?

Leaning forward and squinting into the blurry white scene ahead of my car, I'm relatively certain the answer to my own question is 'I wasn't'.

Isn't there some sort of rule about not making drastic decisions after a breakup? Don't cut or color your hair, don't get a tattoo, don't ditch your long-standing Christmas plans for a random getaway out in the middle of God-doesn't-even-know-where with a hot relative stranger?

Because I *may* have just done the latter.

Okay, not "may have" – I *have* done the latter.

But the thing is, I don't speak to my family anymore, and my usual Christmas plans involve inviting myself to my college best friend's parents' house for their family Christmas. However, this Christmas is Vince's first with his boyfriend, Bear, and I didn't really feel up to being a third wheel.

I'd really liked the guy I was dating this time and had hoped to drag him along with me. But he broke up with me at the beginning of December and, even though it wasn't a serious relationship, I'd kind of hoped we could turn it into one.

See, I have this reputation as a bit of a playboy, but I actually want to settle down. The problem is, every time I bring the idea up, my relationships die a tragic death. I've heard so many variations of 'it's not you, it's me' in the past year that I'm starting to suspect that it is, in fact, me.

My most recent relationship ended the same way. Tanner was so sweet, but ultimately his reasoning boiled down to the same thing as everyone else's: he didn't feel like we were compatible in the long run.

Maybe that can be attributed to how new I am to BDSM and the kink lifestyle. About a year ago, I realized that I was interested in things that are, shall we say, a little left of center. It started with accidentally clicking on the wrong kind of porn and it was like a lightbulb flickered to life over my head. I was super into the age play scene I watched, and then also the pet play scene I watched after that. Seeing men calling other men 'Daddy' and allowing Daddy to look after them in super sweet ways before he pounded them into the mattress had made me come harder than I ever had in my life.

So, I started Googling. It didn't take long to wrap my head around the concepts I was most interested in, to understand the basics of each role in the lifestyle and the usual kinks associated with each. It wasn't long before I wanted to try it out.

I decided that I was best suited to be an age play Daddy or a pet play Handler. As a pediatrician by trade, I think that I've got caretaker tendencies. Plus, I love getting down on a kid's level and playing with them. So, I figured it would be the same with playing with Littles or Pets.

I did a bunch of research into kink-friendly hot-spots in the city and stumbled upon a kink-friendly community center called The Little Community Center. There I attended a Q and A session about the realities of exploring and living the lifestyle. The people I spoke to were not only knowledgeable, but super friendly and welcoming, even though I was a newcomer with zero experience in their world. Through them, I found out about The Grove.

The Grove is our city's largest and most well-appointed kink club. It is discreet to the nth degree: its advertising is mostly word-of-mouth, you can't enter without signing an NDA, and their security system is mind blowing. It also doesn't appear to be anything but a giant warehouse building until you enter through the soundproofed door from the foyer into the main club space. I felt at home the moment I stepped inside.

I spent a few months visiting and meeting people involved in kinks of all kinds before I started participating in scenes. After that, I dated Subs, Pups, Kittens, Littles…even a Bunny.

But I guess all that babbling means that I think Tanner had a point. I haven't fully settled into my own role yet, so how can I expect to commit to a long-term relationship when I haven't fully worked out with which kinks call to me the most?

Which leads me to why I made the rash decision to blow off my long-standing invitation to Vince's family Christmas when Drake (a *super* hot Daddy I know from The Grove) asked me to join him in the mountains. Vince and Bear have only been together six months, but it took less than a week with Bear for

Vince to realize that he's a Daddy through and through.

I'm a little jealous.

Vince hadn't known anything about the lifestyle at all. He fell into his role by complete accident, and he's thrived in it. He loves everything about being a Daddy, and I'm so happy for him, I really am. But…I've been trying for almost a year to find the same spark that he accidentally stumbled upon, and I can't help but think the universe is fucking with me.

Speaking of the universe fucking with me…

The road is starting to get slippery, which only makes me feel grumpier. I considered putting chains on my tires earlier, but the flurries were so light and intermittent that I convinced myself I'd make it to my friend's cabin without an issue.

Now the clouds overhead are darkening and dimming the sky, and the snow is more storm than flurry, so I have to get my stupid chains out of my trunk and fitted to my tires.

It takes longer than I expected. I hate every second of it. I'm freezing by the time I finish because the jacket I chose to wear today was more for aesthetics than function. It's soaked through, what with not being water or snow proof, and is now doing the opposite of its intended purpose. The sky has also gotten darker, and the wind is picking up.

Merry fucking Christmas.

Ugh.

I clamber back into my SUV and pull back onto the road, frowning at the way my engine shudders and chokes before I get going. Nevertheless, my GPS says that Drake's place is only fifteen miles away, so I'm certain I'll make it.

Chapter Two – Drake

My phone rings, startling me from staring out through the living-room window, which faces my long driveway. I was expecting Anson to arrive an hour ago, but so far there hasn't been any sign of him. With the way the snow is coming down, I'm starting to feel unsettled.

We've been running in the same social circle at The Grove for the past year and, when I heard him trying to talk his way out of another Daddy's invitation to join his family for Christmas, I opened my big mouth and invited him to my cabin instead. I don't do Christmas. In fact, I don't do any holidays.

Call me a grinch if you must, but I just don't see the point. There's currently nobody in my life to decorate for or celebrate with, and I can't be bothered making the effort for just myself. That would be kind of sad, really.

And, because I got the impression that Anson wasn't exactly in a festive mood, I figured we could hang out in solitude together. Drink beers, stream some action flicks, and shoot the shit without any tinsel or holly or stupid elves on shelves to be seen.

Even so, I honestly don't know what prompted me to ask him to join me.

It's not like I had any ulterior motives, no matter how pretty I think he is. We're not compatible as anything other than friends. I mean, we're both Daddies. Or, at least, I think he's a Daddy. He's been open about the fact that he's been trying to discover exactly what makes him tick. I respect him for being willing to try a bit of everything while he figures it out.

Maybe that's it. Maybe it's the fact that I respect him, and with everyone else I know paired up and living their lives, and my sister having moved overseas, maybe my subconscious decided it was time to make some new likeminded friends.

It's definitely not the fact that I think Anson's pretty blue eyes are captivating. And it can't be because I think his heart-shaped face and stylishly tousled blonde hair make him look equal parts cute and sexy. *Nope. Not at all.*

He's just a kindred spirit, that's all. I just want to be his friend.

We're both Daddies. I remind myself. *Being anything other than friends would end in disaster.*

Okay, so maybe part of why I invited him is a dumb crush which I'm hoping will disappear if I spend some one-on-one time with the guy. Experiencing just how incompatible we are in a one-on-one setting should hopefully put my crush to bed for good.

I'd like to put Anson to bed...

Jesus Christ, I need these thoughts to stop. It's getting creepy. Maybe after Christmas is over, I just need to get laid.

Pulling my phone from my pocket, I frown when I see Anson's name on the screen. "Hello?" I answer the call and put the device to my ear, rubbing my palm over my bearded jaw. I've let my beard grow out and it's starting to feel lush and a bit wild. "Anson?"

The line is staticky and I strain my hearing, catching pieces of a sentence. "…ice…tree…airbag…stuck."

I'm striding across my cabin's living room before I know it. "Where are you?" I ask, grabbing my coat and struggling into it with my phone balanced precariously between my cheek and my shoulder. He tells me that he thinks he's only a mile from my driveway, which, in this weather, is too long to consider walking. "I'm coming to get you, okay?"

"…car won't start." There's a distinct note of distress in his voice that has me hurrying even more.

"I'll be there in a few minutes," I assure him. "Hold tight."

I'm pretty sure I hear him sniffle and my heart squeezes. *Don't Daddy another Daddy*, I tell myself, even though I'm grabbing my keys with a rescue mission planned. *Just be his friend, Drake.*

It's hard to stick to that plan when I pull my truck up on the side of the road to find him soaked through and shivering. The front bumper of his little red SUV is banged up from where the vehicle has skidded on a patch of ice and subsequently connected with a tree.

"Are you okay?" I ask him as I approach, finally taking notice of what he's wearing. I'm in snow boots, thick pants and a proper snow jacket. He's shivering in jeans, sneakers, and a thin jacket which can't be helping him at all in this weather. "Did you get hurt in the crash?"

His lower lip wobbles, but he shakes his head. I groan when I realize that he's not even wearing a beanie. Or gloves! Does he want to catch his death out here?

I can't help taking charge. "Get in my truck. Nobody's gonna be able to make it out here in this weather. We'll call for a tow after tomorrow once the holiday is over and the storm has passed."

Anson bites his lip and then hurries over to my truck, his feet slipping and sliding under him as he goes. I grab the keys from his ignition, then spy a black duffel bag on the back seat. I grab that, too, before shutting the car and pressing the button on the key fob to lock it. It clicks and the lights flash twice, and I'm satisfied that that's the best we can do right now.

After passing Anson his bag, I climb into the driver's seat of my truck's cab and blast the heat. The drive back to my place is silent, but after we've slowly traversed my driveway and I've parked my truck inside the attached garage to my cabin, Anson quietly says, "Thank you for coming to get me."

His voice is small, and when I look at him, he's staring down at his lap where he's cuddling his bag like it's a treasured stuffie.

"Anytime, bud," I answer, even though every instinct inside me is urging me to pull him in for a hug. "That storm came on fast. I'm just glad you weren't hurt."

Anson nods. His throat works as he swallows. Then he finally turns his head slowly in my direction. His cheeks are bright pink, and I don't know how much of that is caused by the cold, and how much is embarrassment. "I'm a better driver than that, I swear."

Once again, my Daddy gut insists that this man is a Boy who needs my approval and praise.

I have to remind myself that I'm only feeling this way because my mind is desperate to justify my attraction to him.

Clearing my throat, I smile and shake my head. "Black ice is a bitch. It's just bad luck. I don't think you're a bad driver,

Anson." When he shrugs and looks away, a little bit of that Daddy reflex takes over again and I say, "Come on, let's get you inside so you can warm up. I think a warm ba—*shower*," I catch my near-slip just in time, "some dry clothes and a coffee in front of the fire will do wonders."

"Yeah, you're probably right," he sighs and undoes the clasp for his seat belt. "But, um, can I have something else to drink? I don't do coffee."

"Tea?" I ask as I climb out of the truck, waiting until he's come around to walk next to me before I continue, "I think I've got a few bags in the cupboard." I scratch the back of my neck, feeling sheepish. "I can't tell you how long they've been in there, but—"

"Actually, uh, I was thinking more, like, hot cocoa? I prefer hot drinks to be sweet."

I chuckle, leading the way from the garage to the warmth inside my cabin. "What kind of Daddy would I be if I didn't keep a supply of cocoa?"

Chapter Three – Anson

Yeah, this was definitely a mistake.

Why did I ever think that hanging out with Drake for Christmas would be any better than hanging out with Vince and Bear? Sure, Drake doesn't have a Little at the moment, something he lamented over when we were discussing our mutual lack of festive season plans, but he's still got his shit together.

I clearly do not.

You'd think that being a successful pediatrician would mean I'd have my head screwed on straight, but nope. At work, I'm cool, calm and collected. But in my private life? I'm a mess.

I thought I was on the right track with this whole age play/pet play/BDSM lifestyle exploration thing, but I'm feeling just as confused as when I started. Maybe even more so. To hear Vince, or Drake, or any of the other guys tell it, they just felt *right* in their roles.

I've enjoyed playing, but I can't say it's been overwhelmingly lifechanging. There are parts of it that have given me thrills of excitement, though. Like playing cars or blocks with my Little scene partners, or giving belly rubs to my Kittens and Pups. But the other stuff? Meting out spankings or other forms of discipline, having to make all their decisions for them, taking on their stresses and worries…I've had to work hard at that, and I haven't really liked it.

And, yeah, I understand that relationships are hard work, but Vince says he loves being able to take away Bear's stresses. I've always just resented having to take on additional worries anytime I've done it. Like…why can't I give mine up, too, you know?

So, maybe I'm not really that kinky after all. Maybe I just enjoy the porn. Kink is a spectrum for a reason, right?

I'm still morosely mulling this over as Drake leads me towards the cabin's only bathroom. He gives me a brief tour along the way, pointing out the few rooms as we go. The whole building reminds me of every stereotypical hunting cabin in the movies, only I know Drake doesn't hunt. But the walls are all timber, and it's cozy and open-planned, with a large central living-room dominated by a massive stone fireplace, a kitchen/dining space, two bedrooms, and the bathroom.

Even though it's also all timber, the bathroom feels modern and generous. It has a toilet, a large claw-footed tub, a separate shower, and a single sink set into a white vanity.

"I'll get you a towel and grab some clothes from your bag," Drake says, gesturing for me to head into the bathroom. "You're shivering like crazy."

I can feel my lips quirking despite my melancholy earlier musing. If this cabin is the stereotype of any well-appointed hunting cabin, Drake is the stereotype of a lumberjack Daddy.

He's big and broad, with a rounded dad-bod belly and a sexy-as-fuck smile under his copper-colored beard. The hair on top of his head is more brown than it is copper, almost like he's got some sort of ombre effect going from the top of his head to the ends of his beard. His skin is a light tan color, but he's got a smattering of freckles and age spots over his nose and cheeks, and also on his arms, which are visible now since he took his big, padded jacket off and pushed up his sleeves when we came in from the cold. I make a mental note to tell him to make sure he gets his skin checked at least once a year, especially if he's the outdoorsy type. (The existence of this cabin tells me that he is.)

Refraining from mentioning what a natural Daddy he is, I nod and thank him, stepping into the middle of the bathroom to begin to peel off my freezing, soaked clothes.

I've gotten down to my jeans when Drake's hesitant "Uh, Anson?" breaks my focus. I look up, but he's not in the doorway, so I make my way into the guest bedroom next door. He's got my black duffel open on top of the navy comforter, and he's staring down at it with confusion.

"What's up?" I ask, stepping up to his side.

I'm not oblivious to his double-take when he registers my state of undress, nor the way his gaze sweeps over my chest and flat belly. Then he seems to give himself a shake and points at my bag. "I, uh, I went to grab you an outfit, but..."

"But?" I prompt, leaning towards my bag, preparing myself for more bad news as I look in it. "Don't tell me it got wet in the sn—oh, fuck."

This isn't my bag.

Well, no, that's a lie. It *is* my bag, but it's not *my* bag. It's a bag I packed for Tanner when I thought we might go away a couple of weekends back, only he dumped my sorry ass and I never took the bag out of my car. I just tossed my other bag —one that matches this one— in with it.

With a shaking hand, I reach in and pull out the soft, powder-blue footed onesie with the rubber duckies printed over it.

I open my mouth to explain what has happened, but a bubble of near-hysterical laughter escapes me instead. I sound manic, and I feel like I'm officially at my breaking point. "Of fucking course," I mutter when I get my bitter laughter under control. "This is what I get for not unpacking my car weeks ago."

"Hey, it's okay," Drake tries to reassure me, reaching for the onesie, but I snatch it back against my chest. He holds his hands up in the universal sign of surrender, and his eyes are kind when he says, "you can borrow some of my clothes for tonight. I'm guessing you have another bag in the car? We can go back and get it in the morning."

I glance out the window and frown. "If we're not completely snowed in by then."

"If that's the case, we'll work something else out," he responds.

I shake my head. "I can't wear your clothes. No offence, but they'll be way too big."

He shrugs. "It's just us here."

Grimacing, I admit, "I have some sensory issues. I can't…I don't like wearing ill-fitting clothes." I glance down at the onesie and sigh. "At least Tanner and I were the same size." I lean back over the open bag to inspect its contents and groan. "Damn it."

"What's wrong?"

I can feel my cheeks heating up. "Tanner. He, um, he hates wearing big boy underwear when he's in Little space, so I, uh…" I reach into the bag and pull out a thick diaper. "I only packed these in his Little bag."

"Do you think you could go without underwear for the night?"

It's a practical answer, but I shake my head, cursing my pale complexion as my cheeks burn hot all over again. "It's part of the sensory thing. I hate the way it feels. I could sleep naked, but that's not going to help with walking around the cabin."

Drake swallows roughly, and I wonder if he's imagining me walking around naked. Then I remind myself that even if he does find me attractive, there's no way he'd want me. I'm not a Little. Hell, I'm not even a Boy. And I know he's a lifestyle Daddy. It's not just about kinky scenes for him. He wants someone he can be Daddy for all the time, whether they're Big or Little.

He clears his throat. "What, um, what are you going to do, then? How can I help?"

"Well," now that my panic is receding, I'm starting to see the humor in this situation, "I guess I'm going to see what it's like on the other side of the fence, aren't I?"

Drake makes a slightly strangled sound in the back of his throat. "What?"

"It's kind of like when you're training to be a Dom. You're supposed to experience the various techniques you're learning from the Sub side, right?" He nods slowly, but I don't know if he's following my logic. I wave the folded plastic-cotton item in my hand around in the air between us. "This can be kind of like that for me. I'll see what wearing Little stuff feels like for the night."

In fact, I can't honestly say that I haven't been curious about it. Everyone in the age play lifestyle must have at some point wondered, right? Especially about diapers. Like, that's the first thing anyone ever asks about when you mention age play. It's immediately 'so you wear diapers? What's that like?'

Notwithstanding the fact that not all age play enthusiasts are into ABDL, I have to admit that there's a part of me which has wanted to try it for myself. Just once. Just to see if it helps me connect with my Littles better.

Now here's my chance.

"You don't have to do this," Drake says, but his gaze is locked firmly on the clothing in my hands. I'd give anything to know what he's thinking. Has he ever been curious, too? "I can…I can see if any of my last Boy's things are still here. He wasn't into diapers, so…maybe?"

I can't decipher his tone. I don't know if he thinks it's weird that I'm suddenly okay with wearing a diaper and a onesie for the night, or if he wishes his last Boy had been into ABDL or what, but I'm not asking.

"If you want to look while I'm in the shower…" I begin, then cringe and facepalm. "I mean, look for clothes, not look at me."

Drake laughs and the weird mood is broken. He winks at me. "Why can't I do both?"

Despite the fact that I'm still freezing, warmth seems to spread all over me. I'm probably blushing from head to toe at this point. God, I wish we were actually compatible, because flirting with him is fun. "You're gonna have to work a little harder to see me naked."

I grin at his dumbfounded expression and sashay my way back into the bathroom, feeling like maybe Christmas is salvageable after all.

Chapter Four — Drake

I *am so fucked.*

My plan to get to know Anson as one Daddy to another is going sideways fast. How am I supposed to convince my brain to let go of its crush on him if he's going to be parading his adorable ass around my cabin in a onesie and a diaper?

I haven't been with a man in…well, in an embarrassingly long time. My last breakup was brutal and even though I have continued to visit The Grove to play out sweet or disciplinary scenes with Littles or to socialize with other kinky people, I haven't considered getting involved sexually or romantically with anyone.

Well, not until I started looking at Anson like I'm a starving man and he's a Snickers bar.

And now he's planning on wearing that cute-as-fuck outfit in front of me after calling me to come and rescue him…I'm so, *so* fucked.

I desperately search through cupboards, drawers and even the big, timber storage boxes at the ends of the two beds in the cabin, hoping to find just one outfit that might fit my guest, but I come up empty handed. I even dig through the bag on Anson's bed, but the other outfits are just as Little as the one he's taken into the bathroom with him, and he wasn't lying: the only items of underwear I can find are diapers.

There are also a couple of pacifiers, a bottle, a sippy cup, and a pink pig stuffie, too. I'm still clutching the stuffie, toying with the soft, curly tail, when Anson's voice startles me.

"Oh, I see you've met Oinker McOinkface," he says, oblivious to the rapid beating of my heart, "I just call him Oinky, though."

I turn to admonish him for sneaking up on me, but my words die in my throat. The onesie clings to him like a second skin, leaving no inch of him to my imagination. He's well-toned and, if his bare chest earlier was any indication, waxed within an inch of his life under the warm material. He doesn't have a six pack, but he's got defined pecs and biceps, and his thighs appear firmly muscled, too. I'm willing to bet that he puts in a lot of hours at the gym.

But what's really got me struggling not to swallow my tongue is just how Little he looks. His hair is damp and obviously tangled by his attempts to towel it dry. His skin is flushed from the warmth of the shower, no longer pale from the cold. His long, elegant feet are socked in the footed onesie, and he's got the tell-tale puffy bulge of the diaper around his crotch and butt.

He's perfection, I think to myself, wanting to reach out so I can pull him into my arms for a cuddle. Against the pale blue fabric he's wearing, his wide blue eyes seem even bluer and brighter.

He really does look like a picture perfect Little. I know he's recently hit his thirties, but in this outfit, I'd argue that he looks almost a decade younger. It almost makes me feel like a lecherous old man, despite only being thirty-four.

"Drake?" he asks, forcing me to give myself a shake and re-enter the conversation. He tilts his head to the side and smiles. "You okay?"

"How, uh, how are you feeling? Are you comfortable enough in that? It looks—" Amazing. Gorgeous. Sexy. Perfect. "—good."

I die a little inside.

'It looks good?' Could I be any lamer?

Anson looks down at his feet, which he shuffles adorably. I can see his skin flushing a deeper pink again. "It's better than I thought it would be."

What does *that* mean?

Am I just being hopeful, or is there a possibility he actually likes being dressed like a Little? And, if he does, does that mean he might want to try regressing? Maybe some Little play? Using a pacifier? Letting me feed him?

I am getting *way* ahead of myself. It's just a fantasy, that's all. It's my crush putting additional emphasis on the things he's saying, twisting his perfectly innocent words in my head.

Making sure to keep my tone level and light, I cock my head and nonchalantly ask, "Yeah?"

"Yeah," he looks back up at me. "Is…is it weird that I don't hate it?"

My mouth works emphatically before my brain can catch up.

"Absolutely not."

Chapter Five – Anson

I can't help but blink in stunned surprise by just how swift and absolute Drake's answer is. It's definitely reassuring, but he didn't even stop to wonder why I would ask such a question to begin with.

I have to say I appreciate that because I'm currently going through some epic revelations. I'm stuck in my feels big time, or whatever the young people are saying nowadays.

I was not expecting my own reaction to putting on a diaper and onesie.

It was awkward to get the diaper on while standing up in the bathroom, but I managed it, and the effect was instantaneous.

As soon as I tightened those tabs around my hips, something in my brain kind of snapped into place. Physically, it felt a bit odd, having padding around my cock and my ass, making me widen my stance and waddle a little, but it felt…*good*. More than that, it felt *right*.

I'm so frustrated that I can't verbalize it any better than that. It just felt like what I needed in the moment. Like what I've always needed.

There's a weight to the diaper which I found instantly comforting when I put it on. The dry insides of the cotton-plastic blend are soft, but within moments of taping it closed, I discovered that if press down on the front of it, the friction against my dick is like nothing I've ever felt before. And when I climbed into the onesie and did up the zipper, the clingy, warm fabric seemed to mold the diaper against me, adding to the feeling of security while pushing the diaper snuggly against my skin, really enforcing that pleasurable friction.

For the first time since talking to other people in the kink world, I have an idea of what it means when other people said that they just fall into their roles with ease.

Because standing in that steamy bathroom, newly dressed in my onesie and diaper, I felt as though I could quite easily let go and just be *Little*.

It was that very realization that pulled me directly out of the fantasy.

I've never once imagined that *I* might be a Little.

Yeah, I watched Daddy kink and age play porn, but I was excited about being a Daddy…wasn't I?

As the steam began to slink out under the miniscule gap beneath the bathroom door, I had strained my memory and had started to realize that it might not have been the case.

When I watch the porn, I love the way the Daddies look after the Littles. I love that the trust goes both ways, even if it is just a scene for entertainment's sake. I love that the Littles can be vulnerable, and that the Daddies are there to make sure the Littles are safe and have their needs met.

And, as this realization dawned on me, so did the understanding that I was drawn to all of that because I secretly yearn to find someone to be vulnerable for.

I realized that I don't just enjoy playing with Littles in scenes because of my job. I enjoy playing with Littles because I enjoy playing full stop.

Now, as I stand in front of Drake —a man who is arguably the Daddiest of Daddies— and give myself permission to admit that I like being dressed like this, even more is clicking into place.

The reason I don't like doing discipline scenes isn't because I'm a happy-go-lucky, fun-loving guy. It's because I don't feel like I should have the authority to do them. It's because I am more submissive by nature. It's because I would prefer to be put over a Daddy's knee instead of *being* the Daddy.

Holy crap, I'm a Little.

This is not the sort of revelation I want to be having while I'm snowed in in a relative stranger's cabin over Christmas. Especially when the stranger is Drake: the most perfect example of a Daddy ever.

I'm relieved that he's reassured me that it's not weird to like the diaper and the onesie, even though twenty minutes ago I thought I was a Daddy like him, but what might he say if I told him that I've suddenly and unexpectedly realized I've gotten everything all wrong?

What does it say about me that I've been exploring the entirely wrong side of age play kink, and I had no fucking idea I was so far off track? How can I have not understood my own interests and urges? How did I miss all my own signs?

I'm an intelligent man. A doctor, in fact. Isn't this the sort of thing I should have been able to work out about myself?

"Anson," Drake's voice is rumbling and soothing. He places a big, warm palm on my shoulder and leads me over to the bed, where he sits me on the edge of the mattress. "You okay? Talk to me."

My heart hammers in my chest.

I want to talk to him about this, but…what if he judges me for being such a failure at being a Daddy? Because I didn't tell him that I *like* wearing the diaper and onesie, only that I don't hate it. I was deliberately vague because I'm supposed to be a Daddy. I'm supposed to be a Daddy and I'm *not.* I'm supposed to be a Daddy and—

"Anson, breathe for me. Come on, deep breaths. In…that's it. Now out. Good. Good boy. Again."

I hadn't even noticed that I was hyperventilating.

Which one of us is the MD again? God, maybe I should give back my degree, too.

"Are you okay?" As I refocus and my heart rate starts to slow, I blink down into concerned brown eyes. Drake is crouched in front of me, rubbing his palms up and down my thighs. I concentrate on the repetitive, calming motion of his hands and nod.

"Yeah," I answer, but the word comes out all croaky. Clearing my throat, I try again. "Sorry. I, um, I…"

"You don't have to talk about it, honey," the endearment lights me up inside, but he continues, and I wonder if he even realized that he said it, "but I'm going to make a couple of pretty big assumptions. You don't have to say anything, and you can red light if it makes you uncomfortable, but…try to hear me out, okay?"

I swallow convulsively and my heart thuds against my ribcage, but I nod.

"I'm gonna start by saying that if you're comfortable and happy, that's all that matters."

Oh God, he knows.

"Now, I get the feeling you're maybe realizing that you like being dressed in Little clothes more than you let on. And maybe that's making you rethink everything else, too. Am I on the right track?"

Is it written all over my face or something? How the hell does he know that?

Biting my lip, I force myself to nod again, and I close my eyes to try and fight off the unexpected tears which are threatening to slide down my cheeks.

"Can you tell me why that upsets you? Was it just that it was a shock to realize it?"

"I…" Letting out a shaky breath, I look down at my lap and see that he has turned one of his hands over on my thigh, resting it there with his palm facing up. He wiggles his fingers and my lips twitch into the ghost of a smile before I tentatively place my hand in his. He squeezes, and I take a deep breath in, suddenly feeling more confident. "I thought I was a Daddy," I confess. "Or…or a Master or something. I mean…I'm a doctor, and I'm *thirty*, and I…" I blow out a breath and hang my head. "I guess I've had some pretty unhealthy assumptions lurking in my subconscious about the differences between Littles and Daddies."

When I look back up at Drake, there's no censure or judgment in his expression. He just tilts his head in acknowledgement and says, "It's good that you're able to realize that. Working on those unhealthy pigeonholes in your own head is important. But, for the record, I don't think you're any less successful or whatever just because you look freaking adorable right now."

I snort, unable to stop myself from preening under the

compliment.

Drake gives my hand a tug and points at the standing mirror next to the closet. "Why don't you go look in the mirror and see if it helps settle some of your misgivings. You think Littles are cute, right?"

A smile tugs my lips upwards just a bit more. "I do."

"Well, maybe have a look and see whether the guy in the mirror changes some of your preconceived ideas about yourself, hmm? Sometimes we make assumptions about ourselves because we've never considered any alternatives. Have a look at yourself as a Little and see if it doesn't help make things easier to process." He pushes back up into a standing position and smiles down at me with warmth. "You don't have to come to terms with it all at once, either. Don't push yourself too far or too fast. But, while you're looking in that mirror and thinking this all over, I'm gonna go make us some cocoa. Come find me when you're feeling up to it, okay? I'm not gonne judge you for how you deal with this."

As he walks out of the room, I can't help but think that he really is a natural Daddy through and through. He reminds me of Vince, only I realized early on that Vince and I would only ever be friends. But Drake sparks an interest in me that is anything but platonic.

With a sigh and a shake of my head, I decide to listen to Drake's advice. I rise unsteadily to my feet and waddle over to stand in front of the timber-framed mirror, seeing myself for the first time.

Wow.

Drake was right: I look adorable.

That probably sounds conceited, but I look just as cute as the Littles I've played with at The Grove. Turning sideways, I blush and grin to myself at the obvious additional puff to my butt. Unable to resist the urge, I wiggle it, and a giggle erupts out of my mouth at the sight in the mirror.

The overwhelming sense of rightness that I'd felt in the bathroom washes over me again.

I can't fight this, I realize. There's no way I can go back to being a Daddy again. Not after knowing what this feels like.

Standing here in front of my reflection, I see the Boy I've always been but have never known was there. I can feel myself wanting to just let go of being Big Anson and to explore this previously unknown side of myself. Being diapered and dressed this way makes my brain want to just relax into it.

Can I do that? Is that fair on Drake? That's not the Grinchy Christmas he signed up for.

He asked me to come here as a fellow Daddy looking to escape the Hallmark Holiday festivities. I'm sure the last thing he wants is to literally babysit a brand new Little as I explore these new, exciting, kinky urges I'm feeling.

And they *are* exciting.

Despite my freakout, I am *happy* to finally feel like I really do fit in to the BDSM lifestyle after all. The niche isn't what I'd thought it would be, but I want to give in to my body's urges. I want to try being Little.

I've even crossed what most people see as the biggest, weirdest hurdle: I'm wearing a diaper. Should that part have fazed me more, or did it help that I've tried being a Daddy and don't think it's weird that people use them?

Whatever. I'm okay with it, and that's all that matters right now.

Still, I find myself locating my phone from where I left it on the bed next to the duffel bag earlier, calling Vince without even thinking about it.

He's been my best friend since our first year of college, and now we work in the same hospital, albeit in different departments. His opinion matters to me more than anyone else's. Even though I've decided to embrace this newly discovered side of myself, I need to hear him say that it's okay, too.

He answers my call within three rings, which is impressive because I know he's already at his parents' place, and he has his Little with him, too.

"Merry Christmas, stranger," he says, and I can hear the smile in his voice. He also sounds relieved. "I know it's not technically Christmas yet, what with being Christmas Eve-Eve, but I'm surprised to hear from you. Changed your mind about the holidays after all? You know you're still welcome here."

I shake my head, forgetting that he can't see me, and sit down heavily on the bed again. "No," I reply out loud, "nothing like that. I just—" My throat goes unexpectedly tight and tears clog my vision.

"Hey, are you okay?" Vince's voice is suddenly full of serious concern. "Anson, what's wrong?"

In this moment, it hits me that he's always been my unofficial caregiver. When I started looking into the kink, I put the pieces together and saw him as having caregiver tendencies, and I assumed that I was the same, seeing as we're both doctors and all. But now I can see the difference between our professions and our personal behaviors, and I understand that I've relied on him to be a Daddy-type for a long time. Since we met, in fact.

Before I can help it, a sob bursts up out of my chest and through my lips.

That does not calm my best friend down at all.

"Anson, for fuck's sake, what's going on? Where are you?" I hear the jangle of keys and it warms my heart to know that he's willing to come looking for me if he has to.

Not unlike Drake coming to my rescue earlier...

"I'm fine," I tell him, and I let out a watery laugh at his resulting scoff. "No, I promise I am. I just...um..." *Just rip the BandAid off, Anson.* "I just...I-discovered-I'm-a-Little." The confession leaves me in a rush and then I burst into tears again, barely registering the stunned silence coming from the other end of the line.

Now, I've watched Vince interacting with Bear a lot over the past six months, but I've never had his Daddy voice directed my way. It's jarring when his entire demeanor shifts over the call. I can picture him vividly, even though I can't see him.

"Anson, bud, listen to me," he says, using the voice he always uses with Bear when he's calming him down, all patient and warm and loving. It makes me cry harder because I *need* this. "I'm so proud of you, okay?" Another strangled sob escapes me, and Vince shushes me. "No, really. I know how huge and life-altering this is for you." He chuckles, but it's one of his self-deprecating sounds. "Remember when I realized Bear was a Little and he thought I was a Daddy? Remember what you said to me?"

I feel a little guilty because I'd taken his call and laughed my ass off. To be fair, I'd tried to warn him when they'd met at my birthday party, but he hadn't listened.

Nevertheless, the question calms me down enough that I can sniffle and haltingly answer, "I told you that you had a choice."

"You did. And you told me that, if I did go through with it, I should embrace my natural instincts. Well," he pauses to let that advice sink in, "I'm telling you the same thing now. You don't have to do anything with this discovery, Anson. But if you do, just do whatever feels right for you. It's all about feeling good, remember?"

"Fine. Be rational and supportive," I sigh dramatically, making him laugh.

After another moment, Vin asks, "Are you alone right now?"

"In this room? Yes."

There's another beat of silence. "Anson." Vince's Daddy voice is back. "Where are you?"

Exhaling, I close my eyes and confess, "Um. In a cabin in the middle of nowhere with Drake."

"Drake?"

"You know…from The Grove? Big, cuddly, looks like a lumbersnack?"

"Don't you mean lumberjack?"

"I said what I said."

Vin snorts and then seems to do a double take. "Hang on… he's a Daddy, right? I *knew* he had a thing for you!"

Huffing, I shake my head. "Okay, he didn't invite me out here with nefarious intentions, so back down Daddy Vin."

"But—"

"—And he didn't, like, force me to try being Little or anything, either. He invited me here as a friend, and there was this whole comedy of errors which basically ended up with me getting the wrong bag out of my car so then I had to get changed into the Little stuff I'd bought for Tanner…"

"So why not just go get the right bag out of your car?"

I cringe. "So, um, don't freak out, but I had a tiny, insignificant, *super*-minor crash and—"

"*Crash?!*"

"Well, it was more like just a little—" *terrifying* "—skid and a bump against a tree."

"Anson!"

"I'm *fine*, no concussion or anything." I rush to assure him before he gets any crazy ideas about calling an ambulance or something. "So, anyway, my car's a couple of miles away and—" I glance out the window and realize that all I can see is snow. "—we're kind of snowed in now, so…"

"Jesus Christ. Only you would get yourself into these situations." Vince grumbles. My resulting chuckle dies in my throat, though, when he demands, "Put Drake on the line."

Chapter Six – Drake

Determined to give Anson the space he needs to process the discovery he's made about himself tonight, I take my time making us two big, steaming mugs of hot cocoa, using the stove to heat the milk and melt in chocolate, rather than using cocoa powder and the microwave. By the time I've washed and dried the saucepan, I'm getting a bit anxious.

The Daddy in me is telling me there's a Boy in need of comfort and support in the guest room, a few scant feet from the kitchen. But I promised him that I wouldn't push him, and I will not make him uncomfortable.

So, I carry the mugs out into the living room and set them on the coffee table, trying to relax myself with the comforting crackle of logs on the fire. I'm starting to worry that I'll need to reheat our cocoa in the microwave after all when Anson pads into the room, holding his phone out to me. His cheeks are pink again, and he looks down at his feet, mumbling, "Vinnie says he wants to talk to you."

My eyebrows climb towards my hairline, but I accept the device and bring it to my ear. "Hello?"

"Hey," Vince's low, smooth voice is familiar, but we've only spoken a handful of times since he and his Little joined The Grove. He's always seemed like a nice, level-headed kind of guy, if quite protective and possessive of his Little. I guess that also extends to his best friend, though, because he follows his greeting by getting directly to the point. "I don't know what your intentions are, Drake, but Anson's really vulnerable right now. Everyone's always said you're a good guy, and I know he's an adult who can make his own decisions. But I just...I love him like a brother, and this is kind of a huge mindfuck for him, so I—"

"It's okay. Really. I get it." I smile reassuringly, more than aware that even though Anson is studying the worn rug under his feet, he's listening to my side of the conversation intently. "I appreciate that. But you don't have anything to worry about, I promise. I'm here as a friend." I meet Anson's gaze as I speak. "I'm not pressuring him to do anything he's uncomfortable with, but I am also here to support whatever he wants to explore."

Anson smiles and looks up at me from under his lashes and my heart squeezes. I'm in a *lot* of trouble.

Vince's amused chuckle brings me back to the conversation. "You're about to learn that Anson is a 'dive in headfirst' kind of guy. Once he realizes that he's into something, he goes for broke. But, as one Daddy to another, he's more vulnerable than he seems. Shit," Vince sighs, "I should have seen it earlier. I guess he just told me that he was exploring his options as a Daddy or whatever and I accepted it. It makes so much sense in hindsight, but it never even crossed my mind that he might be a Little."

"Because you're a good friend," I reply. "If we went around telling people that we don't agree with the way they identify, that would be pretty problematic behavior."

I feel a stab of guilt as I say it, because I did silently and privately question Anson's kinky proclivities. I've never told him that I thought he was barking up the wrong tree, but some part of me had observed him and thought *'Boy'*, even while he said he was drawn to being a Daddy and a Master. Sure, I'd told myself it was wishful thinking, and I always included him as one of the Daddies, but the niggling question at the back of my brain was always there.

I feel a bit shitty for not trusting that he knew himself. For thinking that I knew better.

The fact that I was ultimately right doesn't make it any better, does it?

"I guess you're right," Vince says. Then, after a beat, adds, "I'm glad he's there with you. If I can't be there to make sure he's okay, I'm glad it's someone like you."

Even as I thank him and end the call by wishing him a Merry Christmas, guilt still gnaws at me.

Anson deserves better treatment than I've been giving him, whether he's aware of it or not. So, I'm going to do what I've just promised Vince. I'll support Anson. I'll help him, and I will be here for him…but I'm doing it as a friend, my crush and excitement be damned.

Romantically speaking, Anson deserves respect and honesty above all else…and I've already failed him on that account.

Chapter Seven — Anson

Should I be more embarrassed that my best friend and my current crush just had a conversation about me exploring Little space? Because right now, I just feel really cared for.

Vince's protective concern lets me know that I'm loved by *someone*, even though it's a platonic love, and Drake's calm, considered response just makes me feel reassured that no matter what happens tonight, I'm going to be safe and looked after.

The very idea there is someone here to look after me makes my tummy all bubbly.

It strikes me, as that thought processes, that I'm actually starting to feel Little. I can't quite describe the sensation, other than my brain feeling lighter. Younger. Sillier. Cuter.

And, let me tell you, I was damn cute to begin with, if I do say so myself.

I'm still stuck on how I could have been so oblivious to the signs that I was exploring the wrong side of the kink. Where being a Daddy involved a lot of focus and effort, this slow slide into regression feels as natural as breathing.

I wiggle my toes inside my onesie-covered feet, giggling at the way the fabric makes the bright yellow duckies move. I wiggle my butt, and I can hear the quiet *crinkle-swoosh* of the diaper underneath rubbing against the material. It is altogether soothing and helps my brain let go of being a grown-up.

After Drake sets my phone down on the timber coffee table, which seems to be made of a log that has been sliced in half lengthways, sanded down, then lacquered to shiny perfection, he points at a big, purple mug with a cartoon elephant embossed on it.

"Your cocoa, sunshine," he says, and my gaze flies to his as my heart beats rapidly.

"Sunshine?"

"Well, between the blonde hair and your bright and cheerful disposition, I thought it was a nice nickname for a Little," he explains. After a beat, he cautiously asks, "Is that okay? I just thought you might find it easier to regress if I called you something other than your name. Not that you have to regress! Jesus," he scrubs a big palm over his face, "you'd think I was the newbie."

"I like the nickname," I answer, feeling inexplicably shy about it. Swaying from side to side, I continue, "It helps. I...I want to see how Little I can get. See where I'm most comfortable. I don't think I've got any hard limits. I didn't really as a Daddy. Um, do you? If...if you're still okay being my caregiver while I do this?"

We're going about this all wrong, and I know it. We should have negotiated beforehand, but how was I supposed to know that wearing the outfit and having Vince go into Daddy-mode on the phone would push me into Little space?

"I am so happy to be exploring this with you," he answers gently. "It's a privilege that you're trusting me with this." Something in the way he says it sounds almost sad, but he keeps talking before I can question him. "I don't have any hard limits, either. Well, no, that's a lie. I don't do CNC or rape play or anything like that, but we're just doing this as friends, so neither of those would come up any way."

I nod, but then I pout, and before I can engage what's left of my brain-to-mouth filter, I'm blurting, "You don't wanna be more than friends?"

Stunned silence ensues.

My cheeks burn, and I'm still adult enough to realize I've royally screwed up. "Shit," I say as Drake continues to blink at me, "I'm sorry. I—"

"Language."

Now it's my turn to blink. "What?"

"You're Little now, right? Or heading that way?" I nod. "In which case, while I'm your caregiver, you're not going to swear. When you're Big, I don't care, but when you're Little, it's a rule."

I nod, biting my lip. "Sorry," I apologize instinctively. "I'll be good."

"I know," Drake smiles at me. "You didn't know the rules. We'll go through them together, okay? But..." he takes a steadying breath. "Anson, I think we need to keep things platonic for now. This is already a huge deal for you. Do you really want to complicate it with...what? Just sex? A fling?"

I shake my head. "No, I...I don't want a fling." Swallowing, I decide to test just how far this 'safe space' logic extends. "I want...I want to find someone who wants to be with me for the long-haul. A boyfriend. A partner. A—" my heart races, because I hadn't known how badly I wanted this until now "—a Daddy. I've been so lonely," my voice cracks and I look down at my feet, trying to keep the tears at bay by distracting myself with the cute duckies, "and I was starting to think the issue was me. And, I guess, in the end it kinda' was."

"Anson…"

I close my eyes against the softness in his tone. I don't want him to pity me.

"Sunshine, come on, look at me." Taking a deep breath, I do as he says. His dark eyes are warm and sympathetic. He smiles gently. "I've had a crush on you since the moment I met you."

Wait…what?!

Drake keeps talking. "But you were exploring various dominant roles and I figured my internal 'cute Boy' radar was off. Wishful thinking or whatever. And that's okay. I was happy just being your friend. I need you to know that I invited you here as just a friend."

"I do know that."

"Yeah, well," he rubs the back of his neck, a sheepish expression stealing over his handsome face, "it didn't stop me from thinking that you were giving off Little vibes, even though you said you were a Daddy. That was wrong of me. I realized that when I was talking to Vince. It was disrespectful to not accept that you identified the way you said you did. Because of that, I think you deserve better than me."

It takes me a minute to do the mental gymnastics to work out what the fuck he's saying, with my brain feeling sluggish with the pull of regression teasing at my consciousness. Then, once what he said all clicks, I laugh my ass off.

"Are you serious?" I ask him when I've caught my breath,

still wheezing and wiping my eyes on the back of my hand. "Jesus, Drake. You think I don't have curious thoughts about people all the time? I do. Everyone does. You're *human*. The difference is whether you keep them inside or not. And you did."

I drop down onto the couch and reach for my mug of lukewarm cocoa, then peer over the top of it. "You *did* respect me because, even though you picked up on parts of me that I wasn't aware of, you kept it to yourself. You didn't interfere with any of my attempted relationships. You didn't try offering me your opinion or advice. You didn't even push me into trying on the Little stuff tonight. You've been nothing but respectful." While I wait for that to sink in, I smirk, "And I've had a bit of a crush on you, too, but I also thought it was weird for a Daddy-type to want another Daddy." I blush. "Guess I know what my gut was trying to tell me, huh?"

I finally sip at the drink he made me, relishing the creamy sweetness and warmth as it hits my tongue. It's all I can do to drink it slowly and not guzzle it down. I don't want to make myself sick.

Drake is quiet, but he sits down beside me on the couch and watches me while I drink. When I'm finished, he gently takes the mug from my hands and sets it back down on the table next to his untouched drink. Then he reaches for my hands and holds them between his much larger ones.

"So…you want to see where things can go? With me, I mean?" His uncertainty makes him hotter and I can't explain why.

I nod.

He smiles. "Okay."

My heart picks up its pace again. "Okay?"

"Yeah. I'd like that. A lot. I'm looking for something long-term, too."

Elation bubbles up inside me and I let out a *whoop* of joy, bouncing in my seat. "I am gonna be *the best* boy for you, Daddy!"

Chapter Eight – Drake

Daddy.

Anson called me Daddy.

I know Vince said that Anson's the kind of guy who leaps in headfirst, and we've somehow gone from 'just friends' to 'let's see where this takes us' in a matter of minutes, but none of it feels like we're going too fast.

Instead, it feels good. It feels right.

"We should talk some more about limits and rules," I say, once the euphoria of hearing my crush call me Daddy has melted into a low thrum of happiness. "Especially if we're going to do this as more than just friends." Tilting my head to the side, I ask, "Are you feeling Big enough to do that?"

Anson nods. "I am. Not gonna lie, getting all snuggly on the couch with you now that I've got a belly full of cocoa is really making me want to be Little, but I'm still Big right now. Or, y'know, Big enough."

"Okay, well, like I said, my hard limits are CNC and rape play. I need you to give your verbal consent any time we try something new. I don't like my Boys to swear when they're Little, but during sex is an exception to the rule. Because we don't know whether you're the kind of Little who wants or needs Daddy to make all of your decisions for you, I won't set any rules like that yet, but I do like to look after my Boys in every way possible. So, I want you to tell me if there's anything you need or want from Daddy. Anything at all, okay?"

"And if it's not something you're comfortable with?"

"That's what safe words exist for. I'll call a yellow light and we can talk about my concerns. But I can't imagine many situations where that might be necessary." After a beat, I confirm, "Are you comfortable with the traffic light system, or would you prefer to use different safe words?"

"Traffic lights work for me." Anson offers me a small, shy smile. "And I'd like you to make decisions for me while I'm Little. All decisions. What I'm eating, what I'm wearing, when it's bathtime or bedtime…Anything and everything, really." He sighs and shrugs. "My day job is high responsibility and often high stress. I resented having to make additional decisions as a Daddy. I should have realized it was because I needed a break from the responsibility in my life, not more of it."

My heart squeezes, but I don't want to focus on the 'should have's of the situation. Instead, I keep the focus of the conversation on our negotiations. "Okay, well, let's start off with me making the decisions and if it's not working for you, say yellow or red and we can talk about it."

"Okay, that sounds good to me," he agrees. "And, um, my hard limits as a Daddy were pretty much the same as yours. I don't really know what my limits as a Little are." The shy smile morphs into something a little more playful. "I know diapers are a major hurdle for some people, but I'm already wearing one, so…"

I can't help chuckling. "What about wetting? Is that a limit for you?"

Anson shrugs easily. He's relaxed and not even mildly ruffled or embarrassed by the question. "It never bothered me as a Daddy. I think, if I get deep enough into Little space, it's probably something I'd do. I really do like the idea of letting go of all my Big worries and responsibilities, even going to the potty."

It blows my mind just a bit that he's so at ease with the concept. I sit back heavily, processing it.

"What's wrong?" Anson asks, turning so he can frown at me. "Is it a limit for you? Because I don't think it's something I *need*—"

"No, no," I hurry to reassure him. Reaching out, I take his hand and squeeze it. "It just means a lot that you're so comfortable with me that you're even considering it. That you trust me so much already. Most of the other Boys I've been with have needed some time to ease into it, even if they've done it with other Daddies before, because it's kind of huge being that vulnerable with someone new. So, yeah, I'm just kind of wowed by how much you obviously trust me."

"Well, you're my friend," he says slowly, "and I do trust you. But…I'm also a doctor. It takes more to embarrass me than the idea of peeing in a diaper. Only," he adds, "I won't use a diaper for more than that. Going further feels more medical than kinky to me, is all."

I nod. "Whatever you're comfortable with. We can just see where this exploration takes you. We've got time."

Anson relaxes again and grins. "I like hearing that."

I still find it difficult to believe that this beautiful man could want more with me than just a holiday fling. If it was anyone else, I'd be concerned that he was just choosing me as the easy, convenient option. But we've been running in the same social circle for a while, and I've never gotten the impression that Anson is anything other than genuine. If he says that he wants to try a real relationship with me, I'm going to trust that he means every word.

"I like it, too," I tell him. "So, I guess the final rules I want to enforce are open communication and honesty. I know it's common sense, but if we're not being honest with each other, it's not going to work out."

The fire is still crackling away behind the metal grate, but it's a different kind of warmth which suffuses me when Anson smiles broadly and says, "You're speaking my language, Daddy."

"Okay, so," my belly flutters with uncharacteristic nerves, "did you want to try finding Little space? Are you happy for me to take things from here? I know you said you wanted me to make the decisions, but is there anything in particular you'd like to start with?"

Anson purses his lips adorably, then looks over at the TV mounted on the wall across from where we're seated. "I know we were both in a Grinchy mood, but…could we cuddle and watch a Christmas movie? A kids one? I…I think I kind of miss Christmas already."

I try not to feel like a failure of a Daddy as I glance around the bare living room. In past years, I've hung tinsel and lights on the walls and stockings by the fire. I don't even have a tree this year, though I do have a gift for Anson to unwrap on Christmas morning. It's impersonal, because I didn't anticipate our relationship becoming more than friends —and certainly not Daddy and Boy— but at least I have something to give him.

"I'm so—"

"Nope," he holds up his index finger and waggles it at me. "Don't be sorry, Daddy. Neither of us was expecting this—" he waves his hand over himself "—when we made plans to hide out here for Christmas."

"Even so," I grumble, wanting to give him a Holiday worthy of his first time experiencing it as a Little, "I could have at least hung some lights."

Anson looks out the window. "The snow's really coming down now. Maybe, if we're stuck here for a couple more days, we can decorate together? Christmas isn't for a couple of days anyway, so we have time and not a lot else to do. If…if you wanna, I mean."

I don't even need to think about it. Pulling him in for a hug, I kiss the top of his soft, blonde head, breathing in the scent of my shampoo. It fills me with a possessive sort of joy, having him smell like me. "I'd like that, sunshine."

Watching him smile shyly when I use his new nickname makes me want to do it again and again and again. It seems to help him let go of his Big headspace, too, because he gets a little squirmy and pitches his voice higher and sweeter when he says, "So…a Kiss-Moose movie, Daddy?"

I pluck the TV remote from the coffee table and then twist in my seat, bringing my leg up onto the couch and maneuvering us around until I'm reclined lengthways on the couch and Anson is lying against me, his back against my chest. Yeah, one of my legs is now dangling off the side of the couch, but we're comfortable.

I get one of my many streaming services loaded up and we start flicking through our options until Anson squeals excitedly and points at the screen. *"A Muppet Christmas Carol!"* He twists his head to look up at me imploringly. "Please, Daddy? That one?"

His big, blue eyes are wide and pleading, his face lit up with genuine joy.

I didn't have any plans to say no, but even if I did, this look on his face would have changed my mind.

He's going to be dangerous when he realizes what that look does to my resolve.

"Of course, sweetheart," I agree easily, and doing so earns me another happy squeal and a tight cuddle. "You like The Muppets, huh?"

"I love them! I grew up watching them. I know all the songs, and probably most of the lines, too. But I promise not to say them. I know it's distracting."

I am not a fan of the melancholy end to his otherwise happy ramble, or the way he's just hung his head and folded in on himself. It's a glimpse into his real childhood, maybe, and not a happy one.

I press play on the movie and wrap my arms around him. "You can sing as loud as you want and say all the lines, sunshine. I want to see my Boy enjoying himself. Plus," I lower my voice as if I'm divulging the most secret of all secrets, "I know all the words, too."

Chapter Nine — Anson

Midway through the first movie, I finally start slipping fully into my Little headspace. It feels almost too easy to forget my adult concerns and to follow the relaxation of being Little. Daddy —and that is definitely how I see Drake as I let go of being Big— makes it super easy to do. He sings the songs with me, doing the character voices and everything. It's such a small thing, but it reassures me that it's okay to be silly. It's okay not to be mature all the time. If someone as big and imposing as Daddy can do it, then I can, too.

My Little headspace makes me feel really good. My thoughts feel kind of floaty, and the grown-up words I keep stored in my mind fade away, just out of my reach. Thoughts become simpler, broken up into clear concepts rather than long, winding trains of logic and critical thinking.

At some point, my thumb sneaks its way into my mouth and Daddy's chest bounces under my cheek as he chuckles softly. I don't remember when I wriggled onto my side, but it's nice cuddling up against him like this, wrapped in his big, strong arms. One of his hands is playing with my hair, his thick fingers carding through the blonde on top of my head, petting me like I'm a cat.

If I was a cat, I'd purr.

Then Daddy asks, "Would you like me to get your paci for you, sunshine? It's better than making your thumb all pruney. More sanitary, too."

That makes me giggle. "I'm a doctor, Daddy. I say it's safe." Then I snuggle in even more closely, not wanting my comfy, Daddy-shaped pillow to leave.

This time, his laugh is louder and his belly jiggles, too. "Pretty sure Little Anson and Doctor Anson would disagree with each other," he teases lightly, then groans as he moves to sit up. "Come on, baby. Up. Let me go get your paci." His tone turns sing-song when he cajoles, "I'll bring back some snacks."

My tummy growls at the mention of food. I sit up and give Daddy my best pleading expression. "An' a bottle of chocolate milk?"

His eyes drift over to the huge, empty mug on the coffee table and then back to me, one of his bushy dark eyebrows cocked in amusement. "More chocolate milk? Has someone got a sweet tooth?"

I grin and nod enthusiastically.

"Hmm." He looks at me and shakes his head. "We haven't eaten dinner yet, so I don't want to fill your tummy up with sugar. So, how's about I get us some healthy snacks—"

"*Blech!*"

Daddy ignores my protest. "—and then after that, I'll get you a bottle of juice or plain milk."

If I were Big, I'd appreciate his willpower. He's doing all the right things and taking care of me the way I would have taken care of a Boy when I was trying to be a Daddy. But I'm not Big, and I'm not impressed with the idea of healthy snacks and plain milk.

Pouting, I fold my arms over my chest and huff.

Daddy snorts. "Anson, you're not going to be bratty on our first night together, are you?"

It's tempting to push boundaries, but I know he's right. I don't want to be punished on our first night as Daddy and Boy, or during my first time being Little at all.

I shift my pout into something more apologetic than petulant. "Sorry, Daddy." The movement on the TV catches my eye and an idea starts to form. Batting my lashes and looking as miserable as possible, I add, "But it's kiss-moose. We can have candy at kiss-moose, can't we, Daddy? Please?"

I know I've won when he closes his eyes and mutters, "Jesus Christ," before he sighs and gives me a hard stare, pointing with his index finger for emphasis. "You are only getting away with that because this is our Christmas holiday, sunshine. I'm not usually this much of a pushover."

We'll see about that.

Even Little, I'm not silly enough to say that out loud. I smile beatifically at him and clap my hands in joy, bouncing in my seat. "Yay! Thank you, Daddy!"

He grumbles to himself as he gets up and heads towards the bedrooms, then he returns and putters around the kitchen as he gets a platter of snacks for us as promised. I watch him work for a little while before I decide to finish watching the movie. The credits are rolling when Daddy slides a big white tray of snacks onto the coffee table, placing my paci and a bottle of juice down next to it.

I narrow my eyes at the juice, and at the various healthy snacks hidden amongst candy and popcorn and other treats on the platter.

"It's a compromise," Daddy says simply. "I don't want to risk making your tummy upset."

"Okay," I acknowledge after thinking it over. "Thank you, Daddy."

"Good boy," he smiles, and the praise makes my tummy do flips. "Now, all of these snacks should be in bite-sized pieces so you can feed yourself, but if you need help, just tell me."

I get a thrill at the idea of him feeding me, but he's right that the foods on offer are all manageable enough for me to pick up and chomp on. I nibble at some of the apple slices first, then the carrot sticks, dipping them in the ranch dressing he put in a cute little container. I giggle when Daddy affectionately calls me a monster because I make a mess as I swirl the carrot sticks around in the sauce.

I snack on the popcorn when Daddy puts on a new Christmas movie —this one an old-school claymation-esque movie about Rudolph and Frosty the Snowman— and I eventually settle back against him with my bottle of juice, after confirming 'green light' when he asked if I was okay with it.

It takes a little practice to get used to drinking from a baby bottle, but it feels freaking phenomenal. There's something soothing about the rhythmic ebb and flow of sucking through the plastic teat, listening to the hiss of air and sloshing of juice.

My eyelids get heavy as my belly gets full. Adding in the warmth of the fire and the steady *thump thump thump* of Daddy's heartbeat at my back, as well as the high-energy of the day as a whole, it's difficult not to go to sleep.

"Have a nap, baby," Daddy says, noticing my predicament.

He gently takes my empty bottle away and leans over to place it on the table. He stretches a bit further to snag the paci and holds it in front of my face, silently giving me a choice. "It's still early. I'll wake you up in a couple of hours for a late dinner, okay? You can stay as Little or Big as you want."

In my sleepy state, I clumsily reach for the pacifier and pop it into my mouth, and I'm surprised by how much I felt like I needed to replace the missing bottle teat. I get into a new rhythm around the silicone nub of the paci, getting used to the mouthfeel, and find that it is almost as good as the bottle. Maybe not quite as satisfying because I'm not getting anything out of it and it tastes more plasticky, but it's still calming.

"Cuddle?" I murmur. The word comes out garbled around the pacifier, sounding like 'cuddoo' instead. I briefly wonder if Daddy understands what I'm asking for. It's too much effort to explain that I want him to stay until I've drifted off.

But he seems to get it because he adjusts his hold on me. "Of course, sunshine."

* * *

I wake up to the quiet sounds of someone moving around the kitchen. The TV is off, and the fire has dwindled down to low flames and embers. The room is much darker than it was when I drifted off to sleep, but still light enough to see because the light from the kitchen extends out this way. Sitting up, I stretch and then grumble as my bladder protests, letting me know that I'm pushing my luck to make it to the bathroom without embarrassing myself.

Except…I'm diapered.

A slow smile tugs my lips upwards.

I'm not going to embarrass myself at all.

Deciding that I'm going to fully embrace being Little, I see my paci has fallen onto the rug at some point during my nap and I scoop it back up, popping it into my mouth with the same sense of satisfaction as earlier. It helps bring back the floaty Little headspace quickly. I decide that I really like feeling all cute like this, able to trust that all my needs are being taken care of and all I have to do is relax.

So I do.

It's a wholly foreign feeling to relax my bladder while I'm fully clothed, and especially when I'm not in a bathroom, but I'm Little enough that I don't fight it. The first few tentative spurts into the padding have me gasping quietly, but then my body can't hold it back anymore and the blissful relief of completely letting go washes over me.

It's hard to explain why, but I feel so free at this moment. Adult rules and social conventions don't apply to me and I am completely, utterly liberated.

Somehow, feeling the padding expand and get heavy while dampness surrounds my cock and balls makes my headspace even more intense. I *feel Little* in ways I honestly can't put words to.

I wriggle where I'm sitting, feeling the previously soft, dry cotton turn kind of squishy, and I giggle at the sensation.

"Well, hello, sunshine. Looks like you've woken up happy." I look up to find Daddy standing on the other side of the coffee table, two steaming bowls of what looks and smells like some kind of creamy pasta dish in his hands. He sets them down on the polished timber and smiles at me. "Did you have a good nap?"

"Uh-huh," I answer, wriggling in place again, unconsciously

prodding and squeezing at the squishy front of my sodden diaper through my onesie.

I hadn't given a lot of thought to what wetting a diaper would feel like, and I really hadn't anticipated enjoying it quite so much.

I'm the littlest of Littles. How the hell did I not know this about myself?

I squirm, my head feeling lighter than ever. I feel excited by how Little I've gotten. It's such a fun feeling, I want to stay this way forever.

"Do you need to use the potty, sweetheart?" Daddy asks, already moving around the table, extending his hand toward me.

"Nope," I grin around my mouthful of silicone as I realize this means I'll get to experience another first, "too late."

Chapter Ten – Drake

*H*ow can it be too...oh.

Oh!

This is even more proof of Vince's warning ringing true. Anson really does just throw himself into things, doesn't he? But even though we spoke about him potentially wetting, I didn't actually believe he would do so so soon.

I've never been with a Boy willing to be so open and vulnerable so early on in our playtime. I'm ecstatic that he feels so comfortable and trusting of me already, but that makes it harder for me to know whether things are going too fast for him to handle or not.

Is he pushing himself out of his comfort zone? Is he doing this for himself, or for my benefit?

Anson's beaming, playful smile sets aside my concerns about that for the moment though. He swishes his hips again and squeezes the front of his onesie-covered crotch, adding, "All wet, Daddy. Squishy, too."

It blows me away that he's not shy about any of it at all, nor does he seem even slightly embarrassed or anxious. I'm so used to reassuring anxious Boys through our first diaper change experiences that it takes me a moment of consideration before I respond.

I extend my hand towards Anson again and smile. "Daddy can fix it, sunshine. Let's get you all dry and cleaned up before we eat dinner, okay?"

He takes my hand and I help him make his way around the coffee table. His gait, already previously widened by the padding of his diaper, is now more of a distinct waddle. It's the cutest thing I've ever seen.

"I've got supplies in my room, sweetheart," I tell him when he hesitates in the hallway, and I give him a gentle tug towards my bedroom door in the opposite direction to his, "come on."

Even though I haven't entertained a Boy in my cabin in a long while, I know exactly where to find my custom designed changing pad, the barrier cream, wipes and spare diapers. Anson watches me with avid interest as I turn the bed into a makeshift changing table, but he cocks his head at me when I turn and hold my hand out again.

"Traffic light, Daddy?"

If I hadn't already had a huge crush on this man, that would have sealed the deal. The fact that he cares about my level of comfort, even while he's in Little space and experiencing God-only-knows how many new feelings, only makes me fall a little harder for him.

"Green, sunshine. Thank you for checking." When he places his hand in my outstretched one, I ask, "And you? Traffic light color?"

"Green!" Anson practically bounces on his onesie-clad heels. "You gotta change me. The wets is gettin' cold and icky."

I want to eat him all up. The cuteness is too much.

"We can't have that, can we?" I tug him against me for a cuddle and kiss the top of his head. I'd love to lift him up, but he's a little too tall and lanky for me to manage it. "Can you climb onto the bed and lie down on the mat, sweetheart?"

He races to comply, his excitement palpable. Without having to be instructed, he lets his legs fall open and nibbles his bottom lip as his big, blue eyes track my movement towards him.

The onesie he's wearing has a two-way zipper which runs from his feet to his neck, and I work it open from the footed end, unzipping him to his belly button. It's an innie, I note, and just as adorable as the rest of him.

There's still no sense of anxiety from him after I've pulled his legs from the pajamas. Instead, he's relaxed on the mattress and is nursing on his paci in slow, rhythmic sucks, studying the ceiling with half-lidded eyes.

"Still green, sunshine?" I ask as I bring my hands to the tabs of his diaper. It's one of the cute, more expensive ones, with a cartoon fox emblazoned on the front and a wetness indicator which has turned the previously blue line bold green.

Anson lifts his head to look at me and smiles around his paci, nodding. "*Yeth*, Daddy," he answers, not bothering to remove his soother. He gives his hips an insistent wiggle. "*Ith* yucky."

The padding has bulged out significantly, so I can imagine the weight and dampness is getting quite uncomfortable. "I've got you, baby."

His head drops back and I peel back the sticky tabs and pull the sodden front of the diaper away from his skin, exposing his beautiful cock. He's half hard, but I ignore his arousal as I remove the diaper entirely, rolling it up and setting it aside to be tossed into the trash. This isn't about sex. This is about taking care of him and letting him explore being Little for the first time.

Later, if he wants to, we can talk about the romantic aspect of the relationship we've agreed we both want.

It still boggles my mind that he wants more than just the next couple of nights. More than just a platonic experience between Daddy and Boy. Even though I know I shouldn't get ahead of myself, I also want to take his declaration at face value. He wants to see if a relationship with me can go anywhere, and I want the same thing in return.

Maybe Christmas miracles really do exist.

My own personal Christmas miracle wriggles on the bed, whining in the back of his throat. "Cold air," he pouts around his pacifier, the impediment turning his 'r's and 'l's into a more rounded 'w' sound, and I want to wrap him up in my arms and squeeze him tight. He's too adorable for his own good. "*Huwwy*, Daddy."

I chuckle and smack the outside of his thigh gently. "Don't get bratty, sunshine."

Nevertheless, I take care to warm the wet wipe between my palms before I run it over his skin, cleaning him up before I apply a layer of barrier cream. He giggles and tells me it tickles. This time, I can't resist bending forward and nibbling at the pale, smooth skin on the inside of his thighs, making exaggerated 'Nom Nom Nom' sounds that only make him squeal and giggle louder still.

Because I'd grabbed a diaper from my emergency stash and not from his duffel bag, the one I slide under his butt and over his cock is plain white, without any cartoon creatures or fancy moisture indicators in sight. It's also not as luxuriously padded as his private stash, either. Anson doesn't complain about the difference, though. Instead, he wiggles his hips and beams at me around the paci in his mouth. "All *dwy!*"

"I bet that's much better, huh?" I ask the question as I wrangle his long legs back into his onesie.

"Yup." He's a bundle of squirming energy as I zip him back up. He pulls his pacifier from his mouth and clutches it in his hand. "Thank you, Daddy!" I barely have time to register him moving before he has pushed himself back up into a seated position and has launched himself at me. With his arms around my neck, he peppers kisses over my bearded cheeks with infectious enthusiasm.

Laughing, I cuddle him close to me. "I just did what a Daddy's supposed to do, baby."

"An' it made me feel good," he declares, popping his paci between his lips again. "I like havin' a Daddy…havin' *you* as my Daddy."

Oh, God, my heart.

Any hopes I had to keep my crush simmering slowly in the background just got obliterated, and my pre-existing feelings for Anson seem to expand inside me. How am I supposed to take things slowly and rationally when he says stuff like that? When he's so content to just barrel headfirst into everything?

"I like being your Daddy," I reply a little gruffly, fighting back emotions. "Even if it has only been a few hours, I know you're the perfect kind of Boy for me."

Anson's tummy growls loudly, interrupting the moment. He blushes adorably while I chuckle and nudge him towards the bathroom.

"Go wash up, sunshine. Then we'd better feed you before that bear in your belly escapes and eats us both."

Anson giggles raucously and does as he's told, while I fold

the changing mat and set the wipes and cream aside. With how comfortable he seems in his headspace, I figure we'll be needing them again.

Taking the old diaper and discarded wipes into the bathroom, I drop them into the little trash can beside the sink, washing my hands while Anson dries his own. After my hands are dry, I guide him back into the living room, where our bowls of pasta are still waiting.

After settling Anson on the couch, I take our food into the kitchen and zap it in the microwave until it's good and warm again, then bring the bowls back to the living room.

"Would you like me to feed you, sweetheart?" I ask as I sit beside him on the couch.

My Boy straightens up and beams at the suggestion, nodding his head with so much enthusiasm that I almost tell him I think it will fall off his neck. He pulls his paci out of his mouth and drops it carelessly on top of the coffee table, narrowly missing his bowl of pasta. "Please, Daddy?"

I'm never going to get sick of hearing the title falling from his lips. Not when it's directed my way.

It's been so long since I've had someone call me Daddy that it almost feels brand new again. The instincts haven't gone away, but I am afraid that I'll do something to fuck this up…which is the absolute last thing I want to happen when I'm being given a chance with Anson.

Reminding myself that he trusts me to take care of him, I shake the distracting feelings of inadequacy off as I get us into comfortable positions, each sitting sideways on the couch so we're facing each other. Yeah, it would have made more sense to eat at the little dining table in between the living room and the kitchen, but this feels more intimate. Plus, it's our

Christmas getaway. If we can't break the rules on Christmas (okay, Christmas Eve-Eve), when can we?

Twirling the fork in the pasta, I lean towards him, his bowl in one hand and the fork suspended over it.

Anson's blue eyes darken as I move the fork towards his mouth.

"Aren't you gonna blow it, Daddy?" he asks with a devious little smirk.

Oh, I love his cheeky side.

I gasp. "How could I forget?!" Even though his meal is no longer steaming, I pucker my lips and blow gently over the loose loops of pasta, watching Anson's Adam's apple bob while his eyes seem glued to my mouth. "Open wide, sunshine."

Anson doesn't need to be told twice, and suddenly it's my turn to swallow roughly as his perfect, pink lips wrap around the fork, taking the offered food carefully.

"Mmm," he says, closing his eyes as he chews and savors his first mouthful of my cooking. "That's nummy, Daddy."

Jesus Christ, he's going to be the death of me.

It's all I can do to keep my hands busy and not reach down and adjust myself. The knowing look on Anson's face tells me he's onto me, too.

Adorable little shit.

He opens his mouth expectantly and I feed him another forkful of his meal. This time, there are less theatrics as he enjoys the bite of food. We do this on repeat until his bowl is empty, which doesn't take long, then I swap his bowl for my own, eating my once again lukewarm pasta while I watch Anson sit back and rub his belly, his eyelids drooping once more.

Just when I think he's drifting off, he asks, "Can I draw a

kiss-moose tree, Daddy? We can stick the picture on the wall an' Santa can put presents under that."

What kind of Daddy doesn't decorate for Christmas? I ask myself again.

"We've got tomorrow to decorate," I remind him, glancing towards the window. It's pitch black out there now, but I'm hopeful that the snow will lighten up overnight. "If we're not fully snowed in, maybe we can even go looking for a little tree tomorrow, too."

Anson nods. "Okay. An' if we're stuck inside, I'll draw a pretty tree."

I don't question him on whether he plans on being Big or Little tomorrow. Like I told him earlier, however he wants to explore this side of himself, I'm here for it.

"That sounds perfect to me, sunshine. I bet you draw the best Christmas trees."

He visibly squirms under my praise, his cheeks turning pink. "You're silly, Daddy."

I really hope that he wants to be with me after this holiday is over, because I'm already addicted to him.

Chapter Eleven — Anson

After Daddy washes up our dishes from dinner, he asks me if I want to play a card game. If I were Big it would be poker, but while I'm Little we decide to play Go Fish. I giggle as he pulls out a bag of peanut M&Ms for us to use as gambling chips.

"You're a total hustler," he accuses a while later, gesturing to my ever-growing pile of winnings. "You threw those first few hands, didn't you?"

I shake my head and pop one of the candies in my mouth, crunching down on it as I grin at him. "This game is all luck, Daddy."

"Don't think that cute smile of yours is going to get you out of trouble all the time, sunshine."

All I take from that is that he thinks I'm cute.

My smile grows wider.

Daddy guards his remaining candies with his big hand, casting me an exaggerated worried look. Laughter, loud and impossible to hold back, bursts out of me.

I can't remember the last time I laughed like this. That I felt so free and light and good.

"You're so silly, Daddy," I tell him and reach for another candy, munching on it happily.

I love chocolate.

"I'm not silly. I'm protecting the last of my funds from the card shark sitting across from me." He leans over the coffee table and tickles me. I squeal and squirm in place.

"Daddy!" I complain through my giggles, "You're cheating!"

"There's nothing in the rules that says I can't tickle you for hustling me."

Somewhere along the line, the cards are forgotten, and I end up straddling Daddy's lap while he sits on the couch. Some time after I got up to tackle him, he stopped tickling me, but he's got his hands on my hips and this feels good, too. A different kind of good to when we cuddled earlier.

A sexy kind of good.

Biting my lip, I rock my hips forward. I can't feel if Daddy is hard, but my cock is pushing against the insides of my padded protection. I let out a needy little moan when I discover how good the friction feels when I rub against Daddy.

His fingers dig into my sides a little harder. "What are you doing, sunshine?" Daddy asks in a strained, husky voice.

"I wanna play doctor, Daddy," I answer coyly, rocking forward again and gasping as I feel the wetness from my precum dampening the insides of the diaper.

Daddy chuckles and then groans lowly when I move again. "We didn't —oh, *baby*—" I can't help continuing to rub my padded crotch against his, and I really like how it seems to affect him, too. But he firms his grip and holds me steady as he gathers his thoughts. "We didn't talk about where we stand on sex during Little time."

He's right.

Swallowing anxiously, I apologize, "I'm sorry. I got excited, Daddy. The rubbies feel too good. What's your traffic light color?"

I relax as he smiles wickedly. "So very green, baby. What's yours?"

"Green, Daddy. I like this a lot."

"What about if I carried you to bed and took off your onesie and your diaper?"

My cock dribbles some more in excitement at the thought. "Even greener, Daddy."

His dark eyes bore into mine. "And what do you say if you change your mind or get uncomfortable?"

"Yellow or red lights, Daddy. I promise."

At that, Daddy leans forward and brushes his lips over mine. It's a gentle kiss. The gentlest that I've ever had. It's barely even a touch of his skin on mine, but it makes my heart gallop in my chest.

Our first kiss.

"Was that okay, sunshine?" he asks me softly, and I have the sudden urge to cry.

It's not because I'm sad, but because I'm so stupidly happy.

This is exactly what everyone at The Grove and The Little Community Center mean when they say they just felt a spark when they worked out who they were inside.

And, yes, I know that sexual interests can evolve over time, but just working out the fundamental basics of my identity has made me feel complete in a way I can't explain, especially while I'm still mostly in my Little headspace.

I feel carefree, liberated, and cherished.

I have a Daddy, and I just experienced the sweetest, most perfect first kiss in the history of first kisses.

Afraid that if I answer him with words I'll ruin the mood by sobbing, I slam my mouth back onto his and kiss him as if my life depends on it.

In some ways, I think it might.

I mean, I know that's dramatic, but I owe this entire revelation to Drake. Without him inviting me here, I might never have given in to my curiosity to wear a diaper and a onesie. I might not have learned that I love being Little. I might not have gotten to kiss the man I had a crush on. The *Daddy* I had a crush on. I might have been facing a Christmas —and a future, *a whole life*— of feeling unfulfilled or like I didn't fit in.

I slide my tongue into his mouth and sigh happily as he takes over and deepens the kiss, one of his hands now cradling the back of my head while we move our mouths against each other.

He tastes like M&Ms and he smells like fire and fading spicy cologne. His biceps are big and firm as I grip them, and his belly is soft where it pushes against my flatter one.

Even though I'm pretty lanky, I feel small against his bulkier body, and I love that. I love the scratch of his beard on my skin, too, even though I know it will give me beard burn if we keep kissing like this.

I'll wear that with pride.

I start shifting my hips again, moaning as the combined sensations of kissing and frotting shuttle through my body. I whine when Drake draws back from the kiss and he chuckles.

"Let's get you in bed before I come in my jeans, hmm? You're far too irresistible and it's been a long time for me."

It's a relief that he's as close to the edge as I am. Even if it hasn't been all that long for me, this feels more intense than any of the sexual encounters I've had since I started exploring kink. We're far more compatible than I was with Tanner or Russ, the Kitten I was dating before him.

How did I miss all the signs? I ask myself again, but I shake the question away quickly. I don't want to end up back down that rabbit hole. Not when I'm about to finally get my crush into bed.

With reluctance, I slide off his lap and rub my crotch, only to have my hand smacked.

Daddy's dark eyes glitter with equal parts amusement and desire when I yelp and look up at him. "While you're Little, you can only play with that when Daddy says so," he tells me in his very sexy Daddy voice. "And Daddy hasn't said so yet."

I want to tell him that rule is dumb, but earning myself corner time while I'm achingly hard is not something I want to do today. So I make myself nod and bite back my brattier urges. We can play like that another time.

I feel another rush of pure joy at those words.

Another time.

Because we both agreed that we're not doing this as a fling. I want a relationship and so does he. I know we still have to discuss it all properly after we've spent the holiday exploring this dynamic between us, but if everything keeps going as well as it has so far, I don't see either of us changing our minds on the long-term thing. And that's perfect.

I'm tired of feeling lonely. I'm tired of my adult responsibilities and all the stress from my job. I'm tired of looking longingly across the club floor at Drake and thinking my crush is weird and out of place.

Seriously, how did I not realize what my gut was telling me?

"Anson, honey, are you okay with that rule?" Daddy asks,

pulling me back out of my spiraling thoughts. I feel my cheeks heat as he gently asks, "Color?"

"Still green. I was just thinkin'."

Even Little, I don't miss the relief in his eyes, or the way his shoulders sag. "Want to share those thoughts? Or are they private? If you're not comfortable—"

"I was thinkin' about how I missed all the signs about me." I shake my head and gesture between us. "I had the biggest secret crush on you and I thought my int-inter-in…" I huff, "my inside feelings were broken."

The big bear of a man visibly melts at that. He gathers me against him for a hug, the warmth of his embrace more than just physical. "You are not broken, sweetheart. There's nothing wrong with not understanding yourself. I'm still learning new things about myself all the time." When I wait in dubious silence, he laughs and says, "For example, I've learned that maybe I don't actually hate Christmas. I just hate not having someone to share it with."

I snuggle into his chest. "I knew it!" I mutter. "Nobody who knows *A Muppet Christmas Carol* back to front really hates Christmas."

He laughs at that. The sound is deep and rich and makes me smile. "It just took finding the right person to bring it out of me. And it's the same with your Little side. You needed to be in the right headspace to discover yourself."

"And with the right person," I add, making sure he knows how grateful I am to have him sharing this with me. "I don't think I would have liked this as much with just anyone else."

"Not even Vince?" He doesn't sound jealous or possessive or anything. Just genuinely curious.

Nevertheless, my nose scrunches at the thought. "He's

basically my brother. I don't think I woulda' liked him changing my diaper or anythin'. Not like I like you doin' it."

Remembering what it felt like to be splayed out on Daddy's changing mat with him taking care of my most base needs reminds me of how horny I was just a few minutes ago. I squirm as my cock plumps up again at the reminder.

"Can you change me again, Daddy?"

His hand sneaks between us to pat my crotch. I'm dry, but hard again, and I push my growing erection into his touch.

"Oh," he says, a knowing smile slowly spreading across his face, "I see."

"Please, Daddy?"

"You don't feel wet," he tells me, and I find the playful glint in his eyes to be a challenge.

Reaching between us to hold his wrist to keep his hand in place, I lock my gaze on his as I force myself to relax enough to soften my erection and void my bladder. I can pretty much always pee on cue, what with my opportunities to use the bathroom at work coming few and far between.

Daddy's eyes widen when he realizes what I'm doing, and I sigh happily at the warm, moist squishiness now surrounding my cock. When he squeezes his hand reflexively, my dick goes straight back to full mast.

Smiling sweetly, I ask, "What about now, Daddy?"

He groans, and the sound is music to my ears.

I bat my lashes. "Please?"

Chapter Twelve – Drake

Having Anson naked in my bed is somehow even more surreal to me than hearing him confess that he was a Little. He's been wiped clean and I've set aside the changing mat and other paraphernalia, and now he's lounging in the middle of my mattress, stroking his hard, perfect cock and staring up at me expectantly.

"Strip for me, Daddy," he demands. "I wanna see you, too."

Standing at the foot of the bed, I'm struck by nerves. Anson's body is everything mine is not. He's toned and firm and hairless, with the exception of his neatly trimmed pubic hair and the fair hairs on his legs and arms. I am literally a bear in comparison, with a thick layer of dark hair over my chest and back and pretty much everywhere else you can imagine. I've also got a rounded beer belly where Anson's stomach is flat and smooth. There are stretch marks on my belly and even under my arms where muscles have turned to fat.

I've been with Littles of all shapes and sizes, but it's been a year since the last time I got naked with someone and my body has changed in that time. Plus, I've been crushing on Anson for months, so I've built up a fantasy of him in my head and even though I know the pedestal I've put him on is just a fantasy, I'm afraid I won't measure up anyway.

I've hesitated a beat too long, because Anson sits up against the headboard and frowns at me. "Traffic light?"

I swallow. "Yellow."

His eyes widen and he reaches for the blankets which I pushed down earlier, just after I stripped him and wiped him down. He settles the covers over his lap before he looks back at me, patting the space beside him invitingly. I walk to the side of the bed, but I don't slide in beside him. I feel restless with anxious energy, so I stay standing, even if it's the more awkward choice.

Despite deliberately wetting earlier —and at some point I'm going to revisit just how hot that almost bratty, and most certainly brazen act was— I know he hasn't been deeply Little since we ate dinner. Still, I feel a pang of guilt to watch him come out of headspace to say, "Let's talk it through."

Don't get me wrong: Doctor Anson Meyers is hot when he's Big, too. But I hate that my safe-wording has interrupted his first experiences in Little space.

"What's making you uncomfortable?" he asks me gently, without any rebuke or annoyance. In this moment, I can understand why he thought he was a Daddy. He is a nurturer, and he does take charge when necessary. "Is it that I was Little? Is it too much for a first time?"

"No, not at all. I'm actually really into sexy playtime with a Little."

Anson's lip quirks and his pretty blue eyes sparkle mischievously. "Noted." After a beat, he asks, "Was it the changing thing beforehand? Would you prefer I go shower?"

Again, I shake my head in the negative. "No. I know you're all cleaned up. I took care of that myself." To spare him from playing the twenty questions game, I sigh and confess, "I just got nervous. You're gorgeous and fit and I'm…well." Sweeping a hand over my torso, I shrug. "And it's been, like, a year for me. I'm out of practice." My cheeks burn. "I'll probably embarrass myself."

He takes it all in, and I'm glad that he doesn't immediately dismiss my concerns as me overthinking or being dumb. Eventually, though, he carefully begins with, "These are totally valid feelings, and I appreciate you being honest with me about them."

I can't help snorting and interrupting, "There's a 'but' there…"

"Yeah, there is." He grins. "My butt is awesome, by the way."

"I agree wholeheartedly." I've wanted to bite it during diaper changes. I could probably bounce a penny off its perfectly taut, shapely form.

"Anyway," he redirects the conversation, probably reading my thoughts from where they're written all over my face, "they're valid feelings, *but*," he pauses and pins me with a very Daddy-like (or, I suppose, Doctor-like) stare, "I'm just as nervous as you are. I've had a crush on you for a while and I never really understood why. And now that I do, this whole thing feels new and different. I mean, fuck, I haven't bottomed since college, for one thing. For another…you're, like, the perfect Daddy. The kind of Daddy I wished I could be. What if…what if I'm not Little enough, or I say or do something stupid in Little space?" He holds up a hand when I move to immediately reassure him, and he smiles with understanding.

"But I trust you, and I know that if I do say or do something stupid, we'll laugh it off and chalk it up to learning about how things work best between us. I mean, sex isn't ever perfect. It's messy, and awkward sometimes, and sometimes you do just have to stop and reposition yourselves or try something different to make the moment work. So what if you come quickly? Is that going to end everything right then and there? I doubt it." His smile turns wolfish. "I figure you'll blow me, or eat me out, or jerk me off, or—"

"Okay, okay," I laugh, even as my cock starts to spring back to life at his suggestive words. "Point taken." Reassured now, I tilt my head at him and muse, "That was very Doctor-ish of you."

"Yeah, well, I don't really have the 'be safe and explore what you're comfortable with' talk with many of my patients. I'm a pediatrician," he adds the clarification for me, which I appreciate.

"Oh, I thought you worked in the emergency department with Vince."

"I do sometimes when they're short-staffed, and I am often on call for any kid-related emergencies." Shrugging, Anson ducks his chin and then looks up at me from beneath his lashes. "But, um, can we talk about that later? I'm kind of hoping I can still get your sexy lumbersnack ass into bed."

I blink at him, bewildered. "Lumbersnack?"

"I said what I said," he grins and throws the covers back again, rolling onto his side and patting the mattress beside him again. "We can just cuddle if you'd prefer?"

I shake my head, my gaze drawn to his cock. It's long and lean like the rest of him, curving upwards towards his belly. It twitches under the weight of my gaze and mine responds in kind inside my pants. "No. I want this." I force myself to look him in the eye. "I want you."

His smile is sinful, and his sweeping glance over my body is heated. "Then get those clothes off and come and get me, Daddy."

He doesn't need to ask me again. I strip in record time, ignoring the rapid beating of my heart as I reveal my soft belly and furry body to him. Anson groans and strokes his cock which seems to visibly strain harder once I'm naked, and the last of my concerns fade away with the physical evidence of his interest in me. Words can be faked, but the pearl of precum at the tip of his dick can't.

"You're so…*manly*," he says as I slide into bed beside him. His hands reach for my chest, winding his long, elegant fingers into my veritable carpet of chest hair. He bites his lower lip and, curling his fingers, gives the hair a tug.

The pleasurable sting of it makes me moan. Anson giggles.

The sound and sight of him sinking back into his Little headspace is yet another relief. Sliding my hand down his side, I tickle him briefly, loving the way he squirms and giggles again. "You're going to be a handful, aren't you, sunshine?"

"Speaking of a handful…" A playful expression crosses his face and I gasp as he wraps his hand around my cock. I' m pretty sure I go cross-eyed when he starts to stroke me slowly. "Is that good, Daddy?"

"Fuck," I breathe, closing my eyes and enjoying the feel of someone else's hand —*Anson's hand*— working me over. "Yes, baby. Just like that."

He smiles and then leans over me, initiating another kiss. Where our first kiss was soft and sweet, and the kisses on the couch were desperate and needy, this one is sure and sensual.

Anson's tongue teases mine, coaxing me to deepen the kiss.

He whimpers as I take control, rolling onto his back while I move over him, reversing our positions. I slot my thigh between his, rutting my weeping cock against his hip and feeling his rubbing and leaking against mine.

"You want to come like this, baby?" I whisper against his lips, "You want to come rubbing against Daddy?"

Anson gasps and arches his back, seeking more friction as he presses his cock into me. "Fuck yes," he exhales, and I chuckle.

"I normally have a rule about swearing."

"You already said it's okay during sex." He whines and opens his eyes into slits, glaring at me. He's still moving and undulating under me when he says, "Plus, cussing makes sexy time more fun, Daddy."

"Is that so?"

He gives me one of his devious little smirks and nods before he closes his eyes and grabs at my ass. "*Fuck,*" he moans out the word as a long, decadent sound of bliss, "more Daddy, please?"

The plaintive begging goes straight to my balls. "Okay," I huff out another half-chuckle, "point taken."

Anson doesn't say anything for a few moments, too lost in our rutting and the slippery slide of flesh against flesh. "Wha— what point?" his question is breathy, issued between escalating panted breaths. "I...*oh*, Daddy...I'm gonna come..."

"Is this how you want to come?" I repeat my earlier question amongst my own ragged breaths. "Or do you want Daddy to suck your perfect cock?"

His eyes fly open and he nods enthusiastically. "P-please suck me, Daddy. I've been a good boy."

"Yes you have," I agree with a grin, forcing myself to stop writhing against him. I slink down his body, peppering his chest and tummy with kisses.

"Your beard tickles," he wriggles when I get to his hip, breathy giggles accompanying the complaint when I kiss him again. "Daddy! You gotta kiss me *lower*." He humps the air for emphasis.

It's way too cute for words, even if his hard cock does look enticing, all shiny where the precum has begun to slide down the shaft.

"Lower where?" I tease, bypassing his groin and nipping at the inside of one of his firm thighs. "Here?"

"Nooo," he wiggles his hips. "Higher up now."

"Oh, I see." I move as though to kiss the tip of his cock, but overshoot and kiss him on the upper part of his Adonis belt. "Here?"

"*Daddy!*" he whines with a bit more impatience, "No! Lower again."

My own dick is aching again, as though it has gone out in sympathy with Anson's poor, ignored erection.

"Where then, baby?"

I glance up to watch Anson turning coy, nibbling his lower lip as a blush spreads over his cheek. "Kiss my *cock*, Daddy," he answers, whispering the adult word in an almost unpracticed way, "like you said you were gonna." He smiles shyly and adds, "Please?"

"I can't refuse when you ask so nicely," I tell him, positioning myself where I need to be. Leaning my weight onto one arm, I use my free hand to grip his base and then ever so gently press my lips to his purpled, leaking head.

Anson's hands fist the sheets at his sides and he bucks his hips up for more.

Licking my lips, I get my first taste of him and swallow back a moan of approval. My own cock dribbles with excitement at the thought of more, too.

"D-daddy…" The word —more a plea— is music to my ears. "Daddy, I need…"

"I know, sunshine," I assure him, moving my fist up and down his shaft. I love watching him falling apart under my touch; the way he gasps and whines and rocks his hips. "But Daddy wants to explore you a little bit more first. Is that okay?"

"Oh *God*," he groans, arching off the mattress again, "yes. Please. More. More of everything."

Accepting the blanket permission at face value, I kiss down his length, darting my tongue out to taste more of his precum as I inch downwards and over his balls. He cries out when I suck one into my mouth, then again when I move to the other. I bury my nose in his trimmed thatch of pubic hair and inhale the scent of him deeply. He smells like the soap I used when I cleaned him off, and that slightly antiseptic scent from the baby wipes, too. But under that is his natural musk and it drives me wild.

Releasing his balls, I trail my kisses lower still, over his taint and towards his furled hole. His breathing hitches and he squirms when I press a kiss there, too, but he doesn't pull away.

"Y-you don't have to…" he stammers when I pull back, the question of his comfort level and consent on the tip of my tongue. "I…I haven't…not since college."

He said something to that effect earlier, too. With my right hand still pumping his cock slowly, I use my left to smooth over his thigh. "Want me to stop?"

I watch him swallow, his Adam's apple bobbing roughly. He shakes his head. "No, Daddy. Just…um…be super gentle?"

The lube and condoms are still in the nightstand drawer, so this gives me an opening to pull away and redirect the conversation back to where we probably should have started before we got going. He whines when I let him go, but I explain what I'm doing and that mostly settles him.

Mostly.

The mention of the supplies I'm grabbing has him tensing and, once I've got them, I sit on the edge of the mattress and hand the little bottle to him. I frown down at the little foil square in my hand and sigh. "Out of date."

Once again, I'm cursing myself for pulling him out of his headspace. He sits up on his elbows and clears his throat. "I, um, I get tested regularly for work. Last test was actually two weeks ago. And I'm negative," he says, "and on PrEP. Y'know, if…if you want to go without. I mean, we're doing this exclusively, right?" He winces. "And we've gone about this all ass-backwards. That's my fault. I get excited then just go full steam ahead." A bitter, self-deprecating chuckle follows and he flops back onto the mattress, covering his face with his hands. "Seriously, how did I miss my Little tendencies? I have the impulse control of a three-year-old."

"Whoa. Okay, firstly, I get tested every six months. I haven't been with anyone in a year, but I still got tested at the beginning of the month, and my results were negative. I'm also on PrEP, just FYI." That's the easy part. Reaching out to pry his nearest hand off his face, I squeeze it as I ask, "Do you want to be exclusive?"

"Yes." There's no hesitation in his reply, but he nibbles his bottom lip again, bashfully. "I don't wanna share you, Daddy."

Oh, my heart.

"Good, because I don't want to share you, either." So, sue me;

I get possessive about my Littles, and just the idea of someone else getting to experience what I have with Anson makes me grumpy.

Anson doesn't have an issue with my admission, though. He smiles brightly back at me. "Really?"

"Really." After a beat, I say, "But we're going to work on your guilt over not discovering your Little side earlier, okay? I don't care how many times we have to talk about it: it's not a bad thing that you didn't see it earlier. In fact," I grin at him, "I'm glad that you're exploring it all with me. It makes me feel really special."

"You *are* special," he insists. "And, really, I'm glad I'm doing this all for the first time with you, too."

*Speaking of first times...*I squeeze his hand again. "You said you prefer to top? Or that you have since college?"

"Uh...yeah." His lip is being abused again, but a sense of foreboding runs down my spine when he looks away, unable to meet my gaze. "I...I didn't have great experiences bottoming in college. It, um, well. I only tried twice. It...hurt. A lot. I..." he clears his throat again and shrugs despondently. "I gave up after the second time. Decided I was meant to be a top and that was that."

There's *so* much unsaid there, so many things that I can assume, and the very idea that someone hurt him —even unintentionally— to the point where he can't even look at me to discuss it makes me rage inside. No, I obviously don't know the whole story or the circumstances, but I still hate the idea of Anson being hurt regardless.

"Honey, look at me," I insist gently, giving him a reassuring smile when he finally swings those beautiful blue eyes back in my direction. "I'm vers. You wanna top, I'm down for it. If you want to avoid penetration entirely, I'm good with that, too. And if one day you feel comfortable telling me the whole story, even if you think it's trivial or just the fact that your partners at the time were drunk or inexperienced, I'd feel privileged for you to trust me with it. But I have zero expectations when it comes to sex, okay? Zero."

His eyes fill with tears and he launches himself up from his reclined position, wrapping his arms around me in a tight hug. "Thank you," he murmurs through a voice clogged with emotion. "And I do want to have sex. I *do* want you to fuck me. I'm not traumatized or anything. I just…I need you to understand that I might tell you to stop. I might just be one of those guys who doesn't enjoy bottoming and I don't want you to be disappointed."

"I couldn't be disappointed with you," I insist, unable to stop myself from wondering about what kind of assholes have put those concerns in his head. "Like I said, I have absolutely no expectations, baby."

"Well, good, because I'm pretty sure me crying all over you has ruined the mood."

"Uh, you're naked and in my lap. There's definitely still a mood."

He laughs, which is exactly what I was hoping for.

"How do you want this to go, sunshine?" I ask him after a little more time has passed, and the embrace has turned into more of a cuddle. "Do you just want to snuggle? Do you want to pick up where we left off? Do you want to fuck me?"

"I want it all, Daddy," his answer sounds like he's sunk back into Littlespace again. While I'm happy that he seems to be able to find it with ease, I make a note to watch him for signs of subdrop, especially after this last emotional conversation.

He wriggles in my lap and I can feel his once-again renewed erection rubbing against mine. "But…can you…can you *try* to fuck me? Please? 'Cause I've thought about it. A lot."

If I wasn't already on my way back to fully aroused again, that quiet confession sealed the deal. Rubbing my bearded jaw along his cheek, I prod, "Oh, really?"

"Mmmhmm. You're this big bear of a man, Daddy. Ever since I first saw you, I thought…well, I thought you'd probably be a natural top. Is that…ster…stair…um…"

"Stereotyping?" I offer. He nods. I shrug. "Maybe, but I don't mind. Most Littles I've been with prefer me topping. It generally comes with the Daddy role." I cock my head and smile to myself as another piece of the Anson puzzle slides into place. "And that probably played some part in why you were originally drawn to being a Daddy."

"Huh," he thinks about it for a moment, "I didn't think of that. But…I'm *really* not a Daddy."

"You can be a Little who tops, though. I'm very happy to experiment." I bounce my hips up to show him just how much I like the idea and he giggles.

"Another day, Daddy. Tonight…tonight I really wanna try the other way around. I wanna feel super taken care of…and, yeah, I know I can still feel that way if I'm inside you, but…"

"Shh, sweetheart. I get it." At least, I think I do. He wants to feel as Little as possible, which means handing over all the reins. It's not a privilege I'll take for granted. "And I'm going to take care of you, honey." I lean back to make sure I can look him in the eye again. "But if you do hate it, I need you to tell me. Call red light and we'll switch things up, no questions asked."

He nods. "I'm so lucky you found me, Daddy."

And there goes my heart again. "I'm lucky you found me, too." Then we're kissing again and the rest of the world melts away.

Chapter Thirteen – Anson

Daddy spends what feels like forever working me open. I writhe on his bed, losing track of time and place. He uses a lot of lube, and his mouth, and he distracts me from the stretch by sucking my cock like he's got an instruction manual on everything that makes me tick.

But, unlike when I was in college, I relax into the intrusion of his fingers. Yeah, it still feels a bit weird being filled up, but it doesn't have the same sense of wrongness that I felt all those years ago. I can't even say that I've used toys over the years, either, because that never appealed to me.

That's probably why Daddy spends so long stretching me out. Aside from the times in college, I've never had anything inside me. My body hasn't gotten used to being opened up or filled up. He's basically working with a virgin hole.

Not that he seems to mind. He's been moaning and groaning around my cock, whispering filthy praises about how good I taste and how tight and perfect I feel around his fingers. That has helped relax me, too.

As much as I'd like to test out being bratty sometimes, deep down, I really want to be his good boy. Especially tonight. It's our first night together, for one. And it's the start of our Christmas holiday. I know the original intention was to avoid getting sappy about the festive season, but now it feels like this whole experience is a Christmas present from the universe. Like, I was driving here and second-guessing all my life choices and now…now I've gotten exactly what I wanted when I first started exploring kink.

I've found myself, and I want to reward my Little side. Merry Christmas, Anson, you've got yourself a Daddy!

And, yeah, I want to reward my Daddy, too. He deserves a good boy for Christmas.

"I think you're about as ready as you're going to be, sunshine," Daddy says, cutting into my thoughts. He pulls his fingers —all three of them!— out of me, and I feel empty in a way that surprises me. "What do you think?"

I suppose I was getting used to my ass feeling full and stretched because I whine and lift my hips. "I'm ready, Daddy."

"Can you roll over onto your front for me? Good boy," he adds when I do as he asks. "And on your hands and knees?"

As much as I'd like to be facing him when we do this for the first time, I know that this position will be easier for me to handle right now, so I comply again, preening when he repeats his praise.

I listen to the click of the cap from the bottle of lube, and I gasp as his fingers breech me again. It feels different from this angle. Not bad, but in the few seconds of reprieve from having them inside me, it's almost like he's got to work me open all over again.

"You okay? Need me to stop?"

I'm surprised to realize that that's the last thing I want right now. I shake my head and rock back tentatively, gasping some more as the stretch becomes more intense. "D-don't stop. Just…*oh!*" I jolt as a burst of intense pleasure hits me out of nowhere. In my grownup brain, I know that Daddy's just crooked his fingers over my prostate, but feeling very Little and vulnerable, all I can say is, "More of *that*, Daddy!"

He does.

It feels so good that it makes me forget the burning of the stretch. It makes me rock back and forth, picking up speed as I get him to nudge that magic spot again and again and again.

This time when he removes his fingers, I complain, "*Nooo…*"

Daddy's laugh sounds a little strained. "Sorry, honey, but Daddy was about to come without ever making it inside you. It was very hot watching you fuck my fingers." Something much thicker than a finger nudges its way inside my rim and my breathing hitches. "Remember, baby, you're calling the shots here. Red light and I'll stop."

Exhaling, I nod. With my eyes squeezed shut, I try to relax, remembering just how much I enjoyed his fingers inside me. If I liked that, surely I'll like his dick.

He takes his time sliding into me in short, slow increments, backing out and rocking back in at what *has* to be a fraction of an inch each time. But the more he does, the more I push back onto him, and it's not until I feel his balls pressed up against my bare skin that I realize he's all the way inside me and the pain is…nowhere near as bad as I remember this feeling.

Yeah, there's an ache and a burn, but none of the stabbing sensation I felt when my college hookups tried to fuck me.

"Is this okay?" Daddy asks lowly, smoothing his big hands down my sides. He squeezes my hips and then starts the motion all over again.

"Uh-huh," I nod, experimentally rocking forward on my knees a fraction, then rolling back again. Daddy makes a strangled sort of sound, and then I realize I'm making one, too. "It's…it's good…" I sound surprised even to my own ears.

"It feels better than good for me," he admits through heavy breaths. "Tell me when you're ready for me to move."

I have to marvel at his self-control. Knowing how long it's been for him, and how tight I must feel, especially when we're doing this without barriers…he really is a patient, caring man. "M-move, Daddy," I tell him and he starts gently thrusting. "S-slo-*oh!*"

My front half collapses onto the pillow, and I cry out as he already manages to nudge my magic spot with his movements. Maybe it was all that time spent stroking the spot with his fingers, so he knew exactly how to angle himself. Plus, it doesn't hurt that his cock is thick, filling me up completely.

"You okay, baby?" he asks, but he sounds smug, like he knows exactly what he's doing.

He proves that he does when he repeats the exact same movement again and again, drawing out more "oh, oh, oh"s from me. Every time he hits that magic spot, shockwaves of intense pleasure skitter through my whole body. My cock is hard and leaking so much I almost suggest that he diapers me again, and he hasn't even touched it.

"D-daddy," I gasp as he propels forward again, my voice muffled by the pillow. I turn my face to breathe and repeat, "D-daddy, I…I…"

Words are evading me. Now that I'm not braced on my arms, but more like a combination of my shoulders and face, I reach underneath myself and grab my dick. I don't even have to move my own hand much, because Daddy's thrusts are moving my precum-slicked cock inside my fist. My balls are drawing up tight and I squeeze my dick to try and prevent the inevitable.

"You've been such a good boy," Daddy pants, his movements growing steadily faster and harder, "you're taking my cock so beautifully, sunshine."

"I'm…I…I'm…Oh! Oh! *Oh!*" I want to warn him of how close I am, but I can't get the words out for every direct nudge against my special spot.

He breathes heavily, shakily, and I'm pretty sure I can feel drops of his sweat landing on my back. Then he asks in a low, gravelly, sexy voice, "Are you going to come on Daddy's cock, baby? Are you gonna make a mess in Daddy's bed with your cum?"

I nod, almost sobbing with how hard I'm trying *not* to do just that.

"Be Daddy's good boy, Anson. Let go. Come for Daddy."

"Oh," I let out the involuntary sound with every thrust, "Oh… *oh!*" I'm too far gone and the pleasure is too intense now. I see stars as my orgasm barrels through me. "Oh, fuck, *Daddy!*"

I erupt over my hand, my tummy and the sheets underneath me. It feels like I cum for hours, and I chase every last bit of the high that I can. I'm dimly aware of Daddy grunting and swearing through his release, too, but it's not until I'm lying on my back and catching my breath that I register the stickiness dribbling out of my ass.

I scrunch up my nose and whine at the sensation, shifting my hips to try to minimize how icky it feels.

"What's wrong, sunshine?" Daddy asks. He's collapsed on the other side of the wet spot I made and is squinting over at me with mild concern.

"I need wipes, Daddy." My answer is plaintive and pouty. "Feels…*blech*."

"Oh, baby, I'm sorry. I didn't think. Hang on." He climbs out of bed and disappears out the bedroom door, but returns soon after with a wet washcloth. When he brings it gently to my ass, I'm relieved to find that it's warm. "I guess this is part of your sensory thing, huh?" he asks me as he wipes me clean. "Not that it's my favorite feeling in the world, either."

I shrug, already feeling a lot better for the quick wipe down. "I've never felt this before, but it's icky."

Tossing the used cloth aside, he crawls up the bed beside me, on the side without the wet spot, and cuddles up at my side. "Well, maybe next time, if you still want me to top, we can use condoms to prevent the icky feeling?"

I find the offer really sweet. How many other guys do I know who would offer to wear a condom if they don't have to?

Shaking my head, I answer, "Nope. I like everything else. Just gotta have wipes for after."

"So…you enjoyed that? It wasn't too painful?" I turn my head to find him studying me seriously.

"Daddy," I say with exaggerated exasperation, but a huge smile gives away my real feelings, "didn't you see how much I liked it? I made a *huge* mess and everything."

He snickers and rubs his cheek against mine. I love the feeling of his beard on my skin. "I'm just checking, honey. But you're right: you are all messy now." He places his hand over my tummy, seemingly not at all worried that I still have a puddle of drying cum there. "I think maybe I need to give my baby a bath."

Chapter Fourteen — Drake

Bath time was a great idea. My clawfoot bath is *just* big enough to hold us both, and I love having Anson's back plastered to my chest, his body cradled between my legs as he splashes in the mountain of bubbles I arranged specifically for him.

"Look, Daddy," he chirps, sounding really Little to my ears, "I is Santa! Ho ho ho!"

He does his best to turn around to show me his bubble beard and bubble hat. I can't help smiling dopily at him. He's just too cute for words.

"Oh, Santa! Are you sure? Your beard almost looks like my beard."

He rolls his eyes and lifts a dripping, bubble-covered hand to point at the precariously perched mountain of bubbles on his head. "Santa hat, Daddy. You is silly."

After the mind-blowing orgasms we'd shared, I didn't think our dynamic could get any better, but this bath has proven me wrong.

It's hard to think that we've only been together for half a day. I'm already so attached to this Boy, it's ridiculous. Now, I know we're moving quickly —even for the BDSM lifestyle— and I know that we're experiencing the intense endorphin rush that comes with a new relationship and fantastic orgasms…but knowing that isn't going to stop me from feeling the way I feel.

Yes, once we're back in the drudgery of our day-to-day lives, we're going to have a lot to work out logistically. We're going to need to work out how to date between our working schedules, and we'll need to arrange a routine to fit in the age play stuff, too. I'm sure we'll clash on random issues as they pop up, and we'll probably frustrate each other when our quirks and habits stop being cute and start becoming annoying.

But the fact remains that I can easily see us doing it all together. We just click so well, it's almost frightening. Being snowed in with him is the best Christmas gift I could have asked for.

I let him splash around in the tub until the water cools too much, and then I get us dried off once we're out. Keeping him wrapped in his towel, I strip the bed and replace the sheets with efficiency.

"Um, Daddy?" Anson swivels his hips, still wrapped in his towel, entertaining himself like a toddler would.

"Yes, baby?"

"Can I, um, stay Little? For sleep times? An' can you read me a story an', um…" his cheeks turn pink and he looks at the floor. "Can I sleep in here with you?"

Am I surprised by any of his requests? Not in the least. I promised him that he could explore his Little side at his own pace, and we'd already arranged to stay here until the day after Christmas, though I am concerned that the heavy snowfall might extend our stay a bit longer. I can't see any reason to rush him into a routine or into facing his discoveries in his adult headspace.

"Of course, sunshine. Did you want me to get Oinky for you?"

He gasps, his blue eyes going wide. "Oinky! I forgotted him!"

"That's okay. He's just been waiting in your room. I'll go get him." I've got to get his bag with his spare onesies and diapers anyway.

Earlier today, I threw the outfit he was wearing when I rescued him from his car into my washing machine, and then into my dryer. I grab them on my way to the second bedroom, neatly folding them and placing them inside his duffel bag before I take it back down the short hall to my bedroom. I assume he will appreciate having clean Big clothes at some point over the next couple of days, but I'm still aiming on trying to get back to his car to collect his actual bag, too.

"Oinky!" Anson makes a grab for the stuffy as I enter my room, and I laugh, tossing his bag on the bed while he hugs the pig to his chest. "Come on, sunshine. Let's get you dressed in your jammies."

"Piggies?" he asks sweetly and, sure enough, when I look in the duffel there's a pale green footed onesie, decorated in tiny cartoon pigs. And I'd thought the ducks were adorable.

"And a diaper?" I pull one of those out, too.

"Yes peas, Daddy."

'Peas'. Not 'please'. The regression talk is going to make my heart explode. I love that he's really letting himself sink into his headspace now, discovering how Little he wants to be, clearly not worried that I'll judge him for the baby talk.

He's comfortable with me.

Has it really only been a day? Not even a full day?

I grab the changing mat, barrier cream, and wipes, then get Anson out of his towel so he can lie down for me. It's a quick process now, and I think he loves being taken care of as much as I love taking care of him. He hums happily, wiggling his feet as I zip him up.

Once I've packed away the supplies again, he bats his lashes and looks like butter wouldn't melt in his mouth. "Bottle, Daddy? An' my paci for later?"

"And a story book," I agree with a nod. "Get yourself all comfy in bed. Daddy will be right back."

When I return from stoking the fire in the living room, nabbing his pacifier and warming a bottle of milk, I find Anson curled beneath the blankets in the middle of my bed. He's got Oinky tucked under his arm and his eyes already drooping.

I hand him his bottle and then pull a story book out from my nightstand drawer. It's always been a favorite of mine, and I've always kept copies in my nightstands, even when I've been single or dating guys who weren't in the lifestyle.

"Oh!" Anson eyes the cover, taking in the fuzzy blue Muppet with excitement. His next sentence is mildly garbled courtesy of the bottle's teat in his mouth. "Da Monstah Adda En' O'dis Book! I lub Sez'me Stweet."

Honestly, I could have predicted that after seeing his excitement over the movies we watched earlier. Still, I smile softly and settle against the headboard next to him, propping myself up with pillows. He dives into the space under my arm and snuggles in, holding his bottle up at an awkward side angle, making it hiss and gurgle as he sucks from it.

Strangely, the rhythmic sound is kind of soothing, so I let it go in preference of reading the book.

And, yes, I do do the Grover voice.

Anson giggles as I start to read, but not even five pages in, he goes lax against me, the bottle drooping from his hold. It's held in place only by his teeth and I set the book aside to carefully pry the half-empty bottle away. I replace it with his pacifier, which he instinctively suckles at, sighing happily.

I don't know what tomorrow will bring, but for the first time in a long time, I fall asleep in a lover's arms, feeling content and wanted instead of lonely.

* * *

When I wake up in the morning, I'm momentarily disoriented. There are arms wrapped around me and a long, firm leg slotted in between mine, the other thrown over my hip. My cock is extremely happy with this discovery, and only grows happier as my brain catches up and remembers yesterday.

"Mmm," Anson mumbles sleepily, stretching and nuzzling further into my chest, the side of his abs grazing my morning wood, "someone's woken up happy, huh?"

"It's hard not to when I wake up with a gorgeous Boy in my arms."

"It's hard alright," he jokes, then rubs his crotch into my hip in reciprocation. Even through the padded layers, I can feel his answering hardness. "And so am I."

I loved having him Little for most of our time spent together yesterday, but it's also nice interacting with him in his adult headspace, too. "Want me to take care of that for you?"

He hums again and then complains, "I've gotta take a leak." The statement is followed by a groan of disappointment. "It's so warm and snuggly in here. I don't want to get up."

"I mean, you *are* diapered," I suggest, keeping my tone nonchalant. It makes no difference to me if he wets. "And the bathroom is probably freezing right now."

I need to get up and re-stoke the fire and woodburning stove which do the bulk of the work keeping the cabin warm. They've dwindled during the night, but I also don't want to leave the warm cuddly bubble we've got going right now. I do have a small space heater which I use as backup for warming the bathroom but getting that running also means having to leave the bed.

Anson snorts. "Yeah…that doesn't really appeal to me while I'm Big."

I sigh. "Guess we're getting up, then. Stay put: I'll go get the bathroom warmed up."

Wearing only my soft pajama bottoms, I slide my feet into the old man slippers I keep under the bed and head into the bathroom, getting the space heater set up and turning it on before I head back into the main living area to get the fires burning in the big fireplace in the living room, and the little woodburning stove in the kitchen. I have ceiling fans turning clockwise to circulate the warm air through the rest of the cabin, and as I shiver my way back into my bedroom, I hope that it starts warming up again soon.

Anson is all bundled up inside my warm blankets, a tuft of blonde hair the only part of him visible as I draw near. Chuckling, I slide back under the blankets, ignoring his protests that I'm letting the cold air in.

"Bathroom should be tolerable by now," I tell him.

He gnaws at his lip and looks down in the direction of his feet. "I'm gonna have to get out of the onesie, aren't I?"

"You're at least going to have to undo it to your crotch, yeah."

Despite being Big, he pouts. "It'll be cold."

I shrug. "Hopefully not too bad now that I've got the space heater going in there."

"Shoulda' just used the diaper," he grumbles under his breath as he begins squirming around under the covers. I hear the zipper of his onesie lowering and I can't contain my amusement.

"You want a hand, sunshine?"

"…Maybe."

He's so cute when he's petulant.

Sitting up, I pull the covers away and he yowls at the exposure to the cooler air of the bedroom. "Come on, get undressed in the bathroom where it's warmer. Do you want to change into your adult outfit from yesterday, or back into your onesie once you've gone pot—er, once you've done your thing?"

"You can still say stuff like 'go potty' while I'm Big," he says as he climbs out of bed, his onesie gaping open to reveal his mouth-watering torso. "It's cute. I like that you're in Daddy-mode twenty-four-seven." He cocks his head. "But I'll go for the adult outfit for now. When I want to be Little again, I want the full 'Daddy, dress me' experience."

"Duly noted," I grin. "I'll grab your stuff. Go pee."

"Yes, Daddy," he responds playfully, then heads to the bathroom. I can hear his sigh of relief when he enters the warm room, and I busy myself getting his clothes out of his duffel.

I feel a slight pang of *something* as I pick them up. It's not quite disappointment or loss, but it's in that vicinity. And it's dumb, because I know I'll see him in his Little clothes again before our Christmas getaway is over. Plus, Anson looks hot as sin in his molded jeans and henleys. I won't be missing out on anything when he's dressed as his usual adult persona again.

But maybe a part of me is worried that, once he is, he'll decide that what happened was a fluke. That he had a momentary lapse of judgement caused by an emotionally intense day. That he was only convincing himself to enjoy the Little stuff because he had no other options.

I know it's unlikely, but it's still a fear simmering in the darkest recesses of my brain.

I'm so used to things not going my way that I can't help waiting for the other shoe to drop.

Maybe it was a bad idea to get so attached to him so easily and so soon after all.

Chapter Fifteen – Anson

Drake passes me my bundle of freshly cleaned clothes and then rambles something about making breakfast. I hum happily and pull my boxer briefs and jeans on, scrunching my nose at how *wrong* they feel after wearing the super comfy Little clothes for the better part of the past twenty-four hours.

And what a mindfuck that is!

I *like* being fashionable. I like looking hot. These are my favorite jeans, damn it.

And yet…they feel too snug and too stiff and too…grown up.

Huh. Maybe I'm not entirely ready to be Big again after all.

But I have to be. Drake did not sign up to be Daddy to someone in Littlespace for his entire Christmas break. That wouldn't be fair to him. Additionally, we need to talk properly about how we both honestly felt yesterday went, and whether we both still agree to an exclusive, serious relationship in the cold light of a new day.

I know how I feel. After waking up in Drake's arms after a night of blissful, uninterrupted sleep, I never want to wake up any other way again.

I know that's a pipedream: we've both got jobs to go back to after Christmas, and we have our own homes…but I'd like to at least wake up in his bed, or with him in mine, more often than not.

Not to mention, I want my bedtimes to all be like the one last night. I want to be cuddled and read to. I want to listen as I'm read a book, and I want to suck on a paci and snuggle Oinky and Daddy.

I want to feel little and cherished as I nod off to dreamland.

I don't want to have to worry about which reports I need to fill out, which pathology tests I need to chase down, which patients' parents are struggling to afford the care their kids need…I just want to lose myself in the special place where my Daddy takes control and there's nothing to worry about except whether I need a change or not. And even then, I don't even need to worry about that, because I know Daddy will check and make sure I'm clean and comfy.

So…yeah. I know how I feel.

But does Drake feel the same way? Or was I too Little for him? He seemed perfectly at ease with the wetting and the diapers, and my baby-talk, but what if a Little who regresses that far is too needy for him in the long run? What if he'd really prefer a Little with a bit more independence?

What if he'd prefer a Little who really just wants Daddy kink with a tiny bit of silly play on the side? There's nothing wrong with that, but after yesterday, I already know that I'm a higher maintenance Little. I want this to be a lifestyle thing with Drake, and not just playtime on weekends, or whatever.

God, I hope he wants the same things that I do.

Once I'm dressed, I head out into the main space of the cabin, relieved to find it toasty warm. Drake is standing in front of the stove, stirring a pan of something that smells delicious. I wander over and take a peek.

"Scrambled eggs?" I ask, and he nods.

"Bacon's in the air fryer, and I've got some homemade sourdough that—"

"Hold up," I blink at him, "homemade bread?"

"Well, homemade in the sense that I baked it myself…at work." He shrugs.

Suddenly, I feel like a dick. I've been crushing on this man for months, and I've never actually asked what he does for work. "You're…a baker?"

I feel guiltier still for the surprise in my tone. Just because he looks like every lumberjack fantasy come to life doesn't mean I can just stereotype him or the work he does.

Drake smiles and bobs his head, seemingly not bothered by my ignorance. "I am, yeah."

"Do you have your own bakery?"

Throwing the tea towel over his shoulder, he leans against the counter to face me. "I do."

"What's it called? Because if it's not set in stone, I vote you change it to Lumbersnacks."

That earns me the laugh I was hoping for, and his shoulders seem to loosen a bit. I'm glad to see that happen, because the weird, awkward tension he's been radiating since I stepped into the room makes me uneasy.

"It's actually called *Making Dough*," he admits, cringing a little as I crack up. "Yeah, I know. I was young and dumb."

"No," I protest. "I love it. Very punny." Cocking my head, I muse, "So…that means you can spoil me with cake and cookies any time I want, right?"

Beneath that beard that drives me wild, I watch his pink tongue sneak out to wet his lips. His dark eyes focus on mine, and there's no levity in his answering question, "Is that what you want? Me to spoil you?"

"Well, yeah, duh." I frown. "You…don't want to?"

He turns away and stirs the pot again, before taking it off the heat. Then he faces me again and says, "I want that more than anything, Anson. But we're moving really fast and I don't want you to feel like I've manipulated you into a relationship."

"Manipulated?" I blink, feeling blindsided. "Why would I think that? Why would *you* think that?"

He throws his hands into the air at his sides. "I don't know. But…you thought you were a Daddy before yesterday. I just…I just don't want you to feel like I pushed you into anything."

"You didn't. In fact, I recall you doing the exact opposite. You gave me other options. You made sure I was comfortable with every single new thing I tried." Bringing my index finger to my chest, I start punctuating my points with little taps against my heart. "*I* wanted to wear the clothes. *I* wanted to use my diaper. *I* wanted you to fuck me. *I* want you to be my Daddy all the time." I need him to understand that he did nothing but support me. "I made those decisions, Drake. Not you. You just helped me realize what I was too oblivious to see before."

His eyes stare into mine intently, his gaze seeming to dart between each of my eyes as he gauges my words and processes them. "And you don't think we're jumping into this too fast? We can still just write the next few days off as a bit of fun experimentation if you want to."

"Is that what you want?" I take a step back, suddenly

understanding that, yeah, I did make all the decisions yesterday. What if he doesn't want this…*whatever it is* to last beyond our Christmas break?

Horror takes over his expression and he moves forward, back into my space. "I want every day going forward to feel like last night…and that scares me, Anson. I've been on my own for so long, I'm afraid I'm clinging to you too fast. I'm also afraid that, once we're out of here," he gestures vaguely around us, "you'll realize you want to experience being Little for someone else, which is totally normal. But if I allow myself to get attached to the idea of being exclusive…"

"You're going to get hurt." I finish for him softly.

My heart hammers wildly in my chest because I can relate to that feeling. Wasn't I just standing in the bathroom having a freakout over the thought that I'm too needy for him?

"Daddy," bringing my hand up, I bury my fingers in the thick auburn hair at the back of his head, "I feel the same way. Like…I was just standing in the bathroom thinking I'd be crushed if you changed your mind about the sweet promises we made last night."

"You were?"

"Uh-huh." I nod. "And I've realized that, at least for now, I'm going to be a pretty high maintenance Little. I feel like I've missed out on so much time exploring who I really am, y'know? And my job stresses me out, so being able to just pretend none of it exists…being able to not have to worry about anything because I know you'll take care of me when I'm home…that thought is heady as fuck. So, I'm afraid you'll think that I'm too needy and clingy, too."

His lips curl into a slow, warm smile and his arms wind around my waist. "It sounds like we really are kind of made for each other, huh?"

My heart goes back to thumping wildly, but not because I'm anxious. Instead, it's because I can feel myself falling for him, which —he's right— sounds absolutely ridiculous after less than a day together. But we're not complete strangers. We were friends before yesterday. Maybe not close friends, but friendly enough that we'd arranged to spend Christmas together. That has to count for something, right?

And who am I justifying this to, anyway? The only people in my life whose opinions even matter are Vince, who fell head over heels in love with his Boy after only a couple of nights, and my sister, who lives overseas and has never really cared about who I'm sleeping with as long as I'm being safe and that I'm happy.

That final realization settles it for me.

"Ignore social convention, Drake," I tell him. "Let's just follow our instincts and see where it takes us?"

He chuckles. "Vince did warn me you were the type to just jump in headfirst. I guess that comes to dating, too?"

"You bet your sexy ass it does." I grin. "I give it two weeks before I'm begging you to move in with me. Or vice versa." I tilt my head, feeling mischievous. "What does your place look like, Daddy?"

"Like a house I inherited from my parents and am slowly renovating myself."

"A whole house? Like…with a yard and all?"

"It's really not as fancy as it sounds."

I roll my eyes. "I'm still living in the first apartment I leased when I landed my job out of college. It's nice, but tiny."

Even though I was earning more than I was back then, I've never seen the point in getting a bigger space. Not when all I do when I get home is sleep. Occasionally I'll throw a party, but even those events have become a once or twice a year event now.

"A house in the suburbs sounds pretty damn fancy to me," I add.

More than ever, I want to settle down. I want to live somewhere comfortable and be a homebody with a sexy man by my side. I want to get a dog and indulge my Little side freely. Maybe even adopt a kid or two at some point, who knows?

Drake snorts. "Are you trying to seduce me for my house, Doctor Meyers?"

"Nope. I'm trying to seduce you because you're hot, an awesome Daddy, and I want you to fuck me again and again and again." I shrug. "The house is just a bonus."

Pink slashes appear over the tops of his cheeks. "How, um, how are you feeling after last night? Not too sore?"

There's a little ache, but nothing worth complaining about. Still, it's sweet of him to ask. "Nope. I think the bath helped a lot with that, but you also spent a lot of time stretching me out. I'm good."

Turning back to the stove, he puts the pot back on the heat and starts stirring again. I think he wanted the distraction, because he fully immerses himself in his task before he asks, "And it was okay?"

Fuck, but he's just so cute when he's all concerned and awkward.

"Better than okay, I promise. And being able to be Little made it even better. Like…I just *knew* you'd take care of me and I just let go and had fun." I pause to consider how he might interpret that. "Not that I don't think I'd enjoy it with us both in adult headspaces, but for that first time, it made it easier to be vulnerable."

Somewhere in the middle of my rambled attempt to reassure him, he craned his neck to face me. Still stirring the eggs, his smile is warm and there's an unreadable glint in his eyes. His voice is kind of strained when he says, "I'm honored that you put so much trust in me, Anson. I really am. I'm not used to…I mean, it's been a while since anyone has. Truth be told," he turns back to the eggs and I am *so* onto that ploy now, "I'm a little scared I'll fuck it up."

"We're probably both going to fuck things up at one point or another. Anyone who says they're in a perfect relationship and never argue are either delusional or lying." I know I sound a little bitter at the end there, but I truly believe that no relationship is magical and without minor —or even major— hiccups. "Once the shininess and novelty of being in a new, exciting relationship fades, we're going to get under each other's skin. We're going to have moments where we miscommunicate, or where my habits annoy you or your anal retentiveness annoys me…and that's okay. I mean, we're not kids, Drake. We know better than that."

"You totally minored in psychology, didn't you?" He teases and flicks the burner off. He also turns the dial to shut the oven down, too, and reaches for the four-slice toaster, sliding down both levers so all of the slices he had ready to go heat at once. Then he looks at me properly again and accuses, "You're far too good at knowing exactly what to say."

"I might have considered switching majors at one point," I confess with a teasing lilt. Then I shrug. "Just because I can talk the talk now doesn't mean I'm always gonna be rational. Talk to Vince: he's seen me have more than my fair share of tantrums when I've had bad days." As my own words register to my ears, my shoulders droop and I shake my head. "Yet more evidence that I've always had a Little side."

"I've seen plenty of grown-ass adults tantrum, and I doubt many of 'em are into regression play," he argues and grabs two plates out of the cupboard above his head and to the right.

"I forgot that your job has a retail component," I shudder, but then I laugh. "You should totally Daddy the next customer throwing a tantrum, though." I put on my best Daddy voice, which does not even come close to his. *"We don't talk like that to people. Go stand in the corner and think about your behavior. Once you've apologized, you can have your cupcakes."*

Drake's laughter is once again rich and booming. "Yeah, sure, I'll give that a go." He starts dishing out steaming heaps of scrambled eggs onto the plates, then pulls the bacon from the oven.

The smell hits me and makes me salivate. I watch, licking my lips as he puts a generous serving on both plates as well, then nabs the toast as it pops up out of the toaster. Lifting the plates, he gestures with his chin towards the square timber table between the kitchen and living areas. It's already set with cutlery, glasses of juice, butter and condiments.

If I wasn't already falling for this man, this is the moment I would have started.

Dinner last night was delicious, and this just proves that he's a man who not only knows his way around a kitchen, he takes pride in what he's serving up. And that's great, because I live on takeout and microwave meals for one.

My stomach grumbles loudly. I blush.

"Hungry, sunshine?"

"Starving," I admit. Then I shake off the embarrassment and bat my lashes at him. "I used a lot of energy last night…and I plan on using a whole lot more while we're snowed in here."

The windows outside reveal that the snow is still coming down strong, and from what I can make out through the sheets of bright white, it looks like the driveway and area is covered in a thick blanket of the stuff. I can't even see the trees out there anymore.

"Yeah…I'm hoping it eases up tomorrow so we can make our way out the day after Christmas as planned. We've still got to get your car out of that ditch."

A bubble of anxiety makes my gut churn and I try to keep the feeling from making its way onto my face. Being reminded of my car and the mess I'm going to have to clean up getting it towed and repaired also brings up questions like 'how am I going to get to and from work while it's being fixed?' and 'will my insurance cover the accident?' and 'how badly is this going to throw out my already unstable routines?' and 'if we're snowed in, how am I supposed to get back to work the day after we were supposed to be home?' as well as other less pressing questions.

It's all adult stress that I just don't want to deal with. It makes me miss the feeling of being Little last night: ignoring all my grown-up problems and knowing that Daddy would take care of any pressing issues.

Pasting on a forced smile, I nod and try to shrug casually, even while my hands shake and my eyes threaten to well up with tears. "We'll deal with that later." I lick my lips as I pull back my chair at the table and breathe in the delicious scents wafting up from my plate. "This looks so good."

Drake leans over from his own spot once he's seated and picks up my toast, buttering both slices for me. As he's putting the last one back down on my plate, he freezes and shoots me a sheepish look. "Sorry. Force of habit."

"I told you; I like that you're always in Daddy mode." In fact, after the meltdown I just narrowly avoided, it helps to settle my nerves. Just having one small thing taken care of for me removes one adult task from my ever-growing list of the things. "Please don't stop."

If he hears the desperation in that request, he doesn't say anything. He just nods, and we dig into our food with a gusto.

Chapter Sixteen – Drake

Anson's been *off* since breakfast. I can't put my finger on how or why, but it feels like he's guarding his interactions with me. Despite our multiple talks about where we both stand, this already feels like he might not actually feel the same way that I do.

Is it possible he just said what he thought I wanted to hear? I mean, we're effectively trapped in my cabin for the next couple of days, so I can understand if he felt under duress.

Oh, God, does he feel under duress?

The last thing I want is for him to feel pressured to act a certain way or agree to a relationship with me.

No. No, he was genuine when he told me that he does want this as badly as I do. I know he was. I could feel it.

But I can also feel him acting strangely now, too.

We've spent the morning playing board and card games with the TV playing random stuff in the background just for some casual background noise. We've talked about some of the people we're both friends with from The Grove and The

Little Community Center, and glossed over our respective backgrounds and families.

He's got an older sister who lives overseas, but he doesn't speak to his parents anymore. He said they weren't the most supportive of his sexuality, and he let me fill the pieces in from there. In turn, I told him that my Dad, who raised me on his own since I was born, died five years ago, and that because of my job and my generally introverted nature, I don't have a whole lot of close friends. It was embarrassing to admit that.

I mean, I get along fine with the two people I hired to help staff the bakery, and I do have some friends courtesy of The Grove and The Little Community Center, but I haven't really made any close connections with anyone since my last breakup. I've actually become more of a recluse because of it, not that the breakup was a bad one. I originally just wanted to give myself some space to recoup and then…well, I fell into the habit of being alone.

It wasn't until I started crushing on Anson that I realized I didn't *like* being alone all that much. Sure, it had its perks sometimes, but…I didn't like feeling lonely.

I slap us together some sandwiches for lunch and we each drink a beer and continue on shooting the shit. It's nice having someone to just talk to about random crap. To laugh and crack jokes and feel as though my company is appreciated.

And, even though he's acting strangely, I do feel like he's enjoying my company.

When he excuses himself to use the bathroom, I think back to my promise to make this place more Christmassy for his Little side to enjoy and I push my own chair back, groaning as my back protests from having been stationary for so long. Then I head into the tiny hallway and stop outside my bedroom, reaching for the latch that leads to the small crawlspace between the ceiling and the roof. The cabin is insulated, so there's not a lot of room up there, but I know I've got some boxes of decorations and maybe even some toys hidden away.

I grab my step ladder from my wardrobe and then climb up until my head is through the square opening. I disturb a bunch of dust, which rises up in small clouds and makes me sneeze, wobbling my footing on the ladder.

"Hey," Anson's voice sounds out beneath me before I feel his hands on my legs, steadying me. "What are you up to?"

I've got my arms through the hole, too, and I reach for the first of the three boxes I can see. "It's a surprise," I tell him, dragging the box towards me. It jingles. That's a good sign.

"A surprise?" he sounds intrigued and amused.

"Yep. Hold on, I'm coming back down."

It takes a little maneuvering, but I get the first, dusty box out safely and turn to pass it down to Anson. He takes it, scrunching up his nose. "It's dusty!"

"We'll fix that in a bit. Hang on."

I repeat the process with the next two boxes, which he quickly sets on the floor beside his feet, next to the first one. He wipes his hands on his sweater and huffs. "Eww."

"Go wash your hands, baby," I instruct, remembering his admission about his sensory issues too late, "and I'll take these into the living room and clean them off."

He doesn't need to be asked twice, scarpering back into the bathroom while I close the hatch to the crawl space and lean the ladder against the wall. Then I grab the two lightest boxes, stacking one on top of the other, and head into the living room. Anson joins me with the third, carried with a towel wrapped around it, moments later.

"Good thinking," I praise, taking the towel from him to wipe the dust off the boxes. "You're Daddy's clever boy, aren't you?"

The moments the words are out, I want to facepalm. I keep doing that! He's not Little right now, but I just can't turn the Daddy side of myself off around him.

His cheeks flush pink and he squirms. "I really like it when you call me your boy. Especially when it comes with praise. I'm gonna need more of that." I watch as his hand pushes down over the front of his crotch. "Turns out it's a thing for me."

Once again, I'm relieved that he doesn't mind me lapsing like that. I grin back and gesture shamelessly to his crotch. "If you were Little, I'd remind you of the rules."

"Good thing I'm not, huh, Daddy?" his smirk turns lewd and he rubs himself, making a show of it for me until his jeans are bulging with the evidence of his excitement.

My bratty little tease.

He doubles down on the teasing by turning his attention back to the boxes. "What is all this, anyway?"

Struggling to ignore my own filling cock, I clear my throat and give the cardboard a quick wipe down with the towel. "I remembered that I had some stuff up there to decorate with, assuming it's not all motheaten."

He doesn't need to fake interest now. Blue eyes gleaming, he drops to his knees and reaches for the folded tab of the box nearest to him and pries it open. "A train!"

I'd honestly forgotten about the little train set. The track is just long enough to set it up to travel around the base of a small Christmas tree. I wonder where I've hidden my stash of spare batteries…

"Oh, Daddy, look!" Anson has already pulled the plastic

engine out and placed it aside, reaching into the box again.

He pulls out a large snow globe detailing a scene outside a building declaring itself Sana's workshop. It's filled with a large, heavily decorated Christmas tree, a couple of elves, reindeer, and a few brightly colored toys. He turns it upside down, prepared to flip it over to watch the snow fall, and gasps when he sees the little windup key underneath the base. Turning it carefully, he flips the globe back over and puts it gently down on its feet, watching and listening in awe as a version of 'Carol Of The Bells' tinkles away soothingly.

"Oh," he sits back on his heels, his eyes misting over, "that's really nice." He gives himself a little shake and reaches for the box again. "What else have you been hiding away, Mister Scrooge?"

Allowing him to ignore whatever the hell that moment was, I laugh and sit beside the third box. This is the one that jingled and, when I pull it out, I find a tangled web of Christmas bunting, lined with tiny bells.

"Oh, that's going to be pretty!" Anson declares, and the higher set to his voice immediately has my focus, even as he seems solely interested in the muddled decorations in my hand.

It strikes me that maybe, as comfortable as he is being Little, he doesn't know how to ask for Little time yet. It's not like we've discussed setting a routine, or how he might want to explore his kink.

"Honey," I ask slowly, "do you want to be Little for a while?"

He nibbles on his lip. "Would that be okay? I know you asked me over to just hang out…"

"Anson," he jumps at how firm my tone just got and I do my best to soften it, "if you want to be Little for the whole time you're here, we can do that. I'd enjoy that just as much as I enjoy spending time with you in your adult headspace."

"It…it wouldn't be too much? Not that, um, not that I want to be Little twenty-four-seven. I just…you'd be okay if I was Little more than I was Big? Just…just while we're here? While it's just us, and the outside world can't ruin it?"

Whoa. Where did that come from?

Something tells me we're going to be having another deep and meaningful conversation before too long.

Before I can assure him, he barrels on, "Because, y'know, I think I'm most comfortable getting *Little* Little, and that's a lot of work for you. I'm really needy, remember? High maintenance? Like, you have to do pretty much *everything* for me, and then there's the changing and—"

"You weren't bothered by me changing you last night," I interrupt, frowning. "Has your traffic light color changed?"

"No! It's still green. *So* green. But…I mean, a little bit is fun and kinky, right? But a full holiday of taking care of my every need? You didn't sign up for that."

I can hear how much he wants to let go. His eyes are tearing up again and his hands are trembling. "You need it, don't you, baby? Need to just let go of being an adult? I bet your job is super stressful, and the long hours probably don't help."

"And I've been trying to be a Daddy…" he adds quietly, and it's a lightbulb moment for me.

"You've been taking on extra stresses and responsibilities for your Boys," I realize out loud. "Oh, sweetheart. No wonder you think I'm going to resent it. It made you feel even more stressed out, right?"

He nods morosely and looks down at his lap, a small sniffle escaping him.

It breaks my heart a little.

"You're not wired to be a Daddy and there's nothing wrong with that. But, baby…Anson, *I am*. I do find relaxation in looking after a Little. No matter how Little you wanna go. No matter how long you need to be Little for. I love helping my Boys —helping *you*— feel relaxed and happy and free. Including multiple changes, if you're really worried about that." When he doesn't respond, I ask, "How did it feel yesterday, being Little and letting Daddy help you?"

Still not looking up, he says, "Good. *Right*. Like…like all the bad stuff was gone."

"Well, that's how I feel when I'm being Daddy." I laugh a touch self-deprecatingly. "It's why I can't turn it off once I've been Daddy for someone. I like it too much to stop."

I can see him swallow before he lifts his watery gaze to meet mine. "Really?"

"Really."

He looks back down at the boxes and presses his lips together firmly before he takes a deep breath, looks back at me and declares, "I think I'd like unpacking these boxes a lot better if I was Little, Daddy."

My heart skips a beat and I push myself back up to my feet, extending my hand to him with a warm, hopefully supportive smile. "And I'd like nothing more than to do that with my Little Sunshine."

* * *

I'm convinced that Anson's earlier tension had something to do with being Big or feeling stressed, because the second I've got him diapered and in his onesie, Oinky's ear clutched firmly in his fist, it has melted away completely. With his free hand, he tugs at my shirt, pulling me towards the living room.

"Come on, Daddy," he demands, sounding every bit like an impatient toddler, "we gots Kissmoose stuffs to unpack."

His excitement is contagious, and it makes me glad that I have some form of 'real' Christmas celebration to offer him for our first holiday together. Next year, assuming our long-term wishes play out, I'll do better. But he doesn't seem to mind the paltry offerings I've got for him now, and I fall into my Daddy role with equal fervor.

He clumsily sets up the train set while I fiddle with the bunting, trying not to damage it as I untangle the knots. I'm distracted by that and don't notice him rooting through the other boxes until there's a spread of Christmas-themed detritus across the whole living room. Flaking tinsel, faded baubles, a couple of smaller snow globes and a few stuffed toys now litter the space. In the middle of the cyclone sits my boy, clapping his hands and beaming at the mess.

"Is like a Kissmoose wonderland," he declares, sounding very proud of himself. Then he springs to his feet and bounces on the balls of them. "Oh, oh! I gots to draw a tree, Daddy! Where's the paper 'n crayons?" He's regressing so far that his 'r's are becoming 'w's again.

I can't deny him anything when he's like this.

That's a terrifying realization to have, and I can only hope he doesn't discover my weakness any time soon. I get the feeling his brattier, more brazen side would have a field day.

"I'll go see if I can find some paper and crayons or something."

My last Little was into toy cars and building blocks more than he liked drawing, so it's been a long time since I had need to stock up for arts and crafts, especially in the cabin. I go digging through drawers in the second bedroom and in my own, then in the kitchen cupboards. Eventually, I find a couple of scraps of old printer paper with random finance stuff on one side of each, a handful of broken crayons and a couple of markers which hopefully haven't dried out.

I place my findings on the dining table and Anson practically squeals as he wraps his arms around my waist. "Perfect, Daddy!"

He plops down to immediately start drawing. I watch for a moment, my heart feeling full. His tongue pokes out of the side of his mouth and damned if that's not something else that makes him far too cute for words.

With him settled, I get him a bottle of juice and some sliced fruit to snack on, then I set about making some kind of order in his Christmas wonderland. In my travels to locate the spartan art supplies, I found some mounting putty and sticky tape, and I put those to use as I decorate the wall beside the fireplace.

My meager decorations look sad and wilted, but I decide it's better than nothing. And, when Anson declares his masterpiece is complete, I help him tape the two halves of his messily sketched blue and orange Christmas tree together, and we use the mounting putty to stick it to the wall above the little train.

"Daddy," his voice wobbles as he steps back to look over the finished product, "this is the bestest Kissmoose ever."

I try to see it through his eyes, but I still feel like he deserves better for his first holiday as a Little. Nevertheless, I agree with him, and make sure to marvel over his amazing drawing.

"Will Santa like it?" he asks.

I think of the six pack of beer and the box of chocolate I bought for him as a token gift, sitting in my wardrobe without any wrapping paper, and my heart sinks again.

"Santa's going to love it, sunshine."

Anson observes me carefully through narrowed eyes before he shakes the entirely-too-Big for his current headspace expression off his face. He hugs me again and declares, "He's already gotted me my present. I got a Daddy for Kissmoose."

And, just like that, my heart gives up pretending that I haven't completely fallen for him already, and I start formulating a plan to make this right.

Chapter Seventeen – Anson

I wake up on Christmas Day snuggled up against Daddy like I did yesterday. After he told me it was okay to regress again, we had the most magical evening and night. He made soup with fresh, crusty, home-made bread rolls for dinner, and I loved that he spoon fed the whole bowl to me before we took another bath together and then settled down for a book and bottle in bed.

He even turned me down when I tried to initiate sex, thinking that he should be rewarded for being an amazing Daddy and giving me a Christmas I won't ever forget. He told me that just because we were going to bed, we didn't have to do more than snuggle unless I really wanted some grown-up touches, and, when I really thought about it, I didn't.

Yes, the thought of getting naked with him got me hard and worked up, but I wanted to experience a night of pure regression, too. When I admitted that I preferred the latter, he didn't seem at all frustrated or annoyed. He just kissed the top of my head and said there would be plenty of time for sex later.

Remembering the conviction in those words makes my stomach all fluttery and I squirm.

"I told you yesterday," Daddy grumbles good-naturedly, his voice a deep rumble above my head, "use your diaper. It's Christmas Day. I want a sleep in."

I snort. "I wasn't squirming because of that." Although, now that he's mentioned it, I could pee.

"No?"

Shaking my head, I snuggle closer into his warm, furry chest and belly. I love how soft and cuddly he is. He's got the perfect Daddy body and he smells faintly of last night's bubble bath. "Nope. I was thinking about how amazing yesterday was, and how you made it clear that we really are going to keep doing this —keep dating and being Daddy and Boy— after the holiday."

His arms tighten around me, and his reply comes out gruff, whether from being sleepy or emotional, I can't completely tell. "You deserve a better Christmas than this for your first time being Little, honey. You deserve presents under the tree for your Little side. Hell, you deserve an actual tree—"

"Hey," I interrupt playfully, "what's wrong with the one I drew?"

He laughs, then sighs. "Nothing. It's perfect and we'll keep it and put it up every Christmas we spend together—" I wonder if he can hear my heart hammering at that casual proclamation "—but I want to give you more than this. I want to spoil you and make up for all the time you spent spoiling Boys and suppressing your instincts, even though you didn't know you were doing it."

"Well, like you said, we've got time to do that, too." I get all squirmy again as the butterflies in my belly take flight. The idea that we'll still be like this next Christmas, even if it is just dream right now, makes me very happy.

And, yeah, I think I really do need to pee.

"Mmm," he murmurs and kisses the top of my head, "Good. Now, sleep, baby. We can be serious again later."

So, the man who gets up stupidly early every day to run a bakery is not a morning person. That's good to know.

It doesn't help my bladder predicament, though. Especially not when he starts snoring lightly and traps me in his big, bear arms, one of his thick legs thrown over my waist, pinning me down.

I suck my lower lip into my mouth and consider my options.

The only one that really makes sense in the end is to regress and let Daddy take care of me when he wakes up. In fact, the more I consider it, the better the idea sounds.

So I carefully dig around for my pacifier, finding it wedged under the pillow under my cheek, and I pop it into my mouth.

It's crazy how, in less than two full days, just the sensation of doing that triggers something in my brain to let go. It's easy to feel Little when I'm nursing on my paci, listening to the rhythmic clicking-sucking sound I make. And being snuggly in Daddy's arms helps, too. He's so big and burly that I *feel* small when he holds me.

My eyelids droop and I forget all about my nagging bladder... until the warm wetness of my unexpected release makes me jolt awake.

Whoops.

Well, not really whoops. Daddy said it was okay. I just startled myself. I was so Little that I didn't realize it was gonna happen...and I want that floaty happy feeling back.

Daddy snores a bit louder and tugs me even closer against him, and that helps me go back to that place where I feel safe and taken care of. Sucking on my paci, I bury my chest in his sweet-scented chest hair and close my eyes.

Daddy will take care of everything.

If only I could have that all the time.

* * *

We wake up late and, even though I wake up wet, I'm Big, so I decline Drake's offer to change me. Instead, I waddle into the bathroom and undress myself, disposing of the diaper before giving Drake the all clear to join me in a lazy, mid-morning shower.

We take our time soaping each other up, exchanging hand jobs beneath the cascade of deliciously hot water. Drake's body bracket's mine against the laminate sheet wall as he kisses me under the spray, and I gasp and whimper into his mouth, still amazed at the turn my life has taken.

He takes both our dicks in his large hand and jerks them together, and our moans combine and echo in the steam-filled chamber of the shower.

"You fit so perfectly against me," he mutters, the words barely audible under the rushing water. "I love how you feel. How you taste." Punctuating that assertion with another kiss, he jacks us a little harder. "How you sound."

"D-Drake," I stammer over his name, already teetering on the edge of what promises to be another mind melting orgasm with him, "you...I...*fuck*."

He chuckles, but the sound is breathy, as if he's just as close to coming as I am. "You're being such a good boy for me, Anson.

Are you going to come for me?"

Losing the ability to form words, I nod vigorously.

"That's it. Be my good boy. Come for Daddy, baby."

The fact that he knows how much I enjoy him being Daddy even when I'm Big warms me from my head to my toes. And the sweetly murmured praise pushes me over the precipice, giving me permission to erupt over his fist in jerky spurts, a series of "Oh God, oh Daddy, oh fuck"s accompanying every shot.

"*Nnngh*, yes, baby. You are so fucking pretty when you come," he declares, shuttling his fist even faster. My cock is getting a little hypersensitive now that I've already come, but I don't want him to let go. I want him to come all over me, too.

"I want to see you come, too," I reply, still a little shaky following my release. "Cover my cock with your cum, Daddy. Mark your territory."

"Fuck that's hot," Drake groans, then, moments later, moans out his own orgasm with a long, low, "*Fuuuuuck*."

He slumps against me, cooling his forehead on the wall behind me while he catches his breath, and we allow the water running down our bodies to wash away the evidence of our activities.

"That was…" he starts, sounding dazed and satisfied, and I laugh.

"Uh-huh," I agree. "Merry Christmas, Daddy."

It really is the perfect way to start the day, if I do say so myself.

* * *

I help Drake make brunch and we take the mixture of breakfast and lunch foods over to the coffee table in front of the fireplace, where I smile at the decorations we put up yesterday. Now that I'm Big, I can understand why he seemed so disappointed that they were a bit threadbare and spartan, but the sheer joy I experienced in unpacking the boxes and helping him set it all up makes it seem far better than any decadent Christmas scene could possibly be.

Beneath my messy drawing of a tree, there are two items with tinsel haphazardly thrown over them. They weren't there when we went to bed last night, and I cock my head as I look at them.

"Uh," I start, ignoring the croissant Drake baked for me in preference of pointing towards the strange new additions, "what's that?"

He cringes and blushes. "It's…I mean, when I thought we were just going to hang out as two Grinchy guys, I…um…well, I still wanted to get you a token gift because it's still *Christmas*, y'know? But now you're my Boy and…ugh, I wish I'd gotten you something better."

He barely gets halfway through his rambled explanation before I'm scrambling over to our 'tree', dusting the tinsel off a six pack of beer and a box of chocolates. I leave the mess of his improvised wrapping paper behind as I carry my prizes back over to the couch.

I bend to kiss his lips softly and place them on the table. "I love them," I tell him honestly. Then my face falls. "But…the thank you gift I got you is in my car. In my other bag." The one that got left behind. "I'm sorry, I don't have anything to give you. At least, not until the weather clears."

The snow has started to let up, but neither of us want to brave the driveway or roads just yet. Hopefully we'll be able to leave tomorrow, though. The thought of having to call the hospital and tell them I can't come back to work after my designated leave days stresses me out.

"Are you kidding?" Drake asks me, sounding completely bewildered. "Anson...you've already given me the most precious gifts I could have asked for. Not just the time spent as Daddy and Boy —or the sex— but your trust. Your affection. Hell, just having company over a holiday I was dreading..." He tugs me into his lap and hugs me tightly. "I don't need material things. I'm just happy to have shared this with you."

Just like that, my stress begins to dissolve again. The worry is still there at the back of my brain, but I'm bolstered by Drake's words. Coming here, spending Christmas with him, even at the risk of being snowed in...it was the right decision. As much as I genuinely love my job, it shouldn't be the only priority in my life. Not when I've got a chance for true happiness. And, really, if I do get stuck here and they freak out about it, it's not like there aren't other places I can work. I could even start my own private practice if I wanted to...

But my thoughts are going wildly off course and I force myself to stop thinking about all the things that could go wrong. Instead, I think about what has gone right.

I've found someone who wants all the same things in life that I do. He wants to take care of me, and I want to make him happy, too. I've finally felt the puzzle pieces over why I was drawn to the age play lifestyle all click into place. I've been able to let go and have the first truly relaxing holiday of my adult life...and I think I may just be falling in love, however fast it might be.

With absolutely zero facetiousness, I settle down on the couch next to Drake and think:

Merry Christmas to me.

Chapter Eighteen – Drake

Christmas Day is spent in a blur of good food and even better company. Anson and I settle in to watch more Christmas movies, tell each other stories from our childhoods (which start as Christmas stories, then move into birthdays and random events), and we send and respond to messages from friends and colleagues, too. After a call with Vince, who does his best not to pry about Anson's kink exploration as he wishes us both a Merry Christmas, Anson asks if he can be Little for a while. I am more than happy for that to happen, feeling a pang of melancholy that tonight will be our last night spent here.

The snow has stopped falling and the sun came out earlier, which was both a relief and a disappointment. I would have loved to have the excuse to stay in this little bubble of kinky domestic bliss for a while longer, but we do have jobs to return to and lives to reclaim outside these cozy timber walls.

I'm equal parts anxious and excited for that. Anxious because I know I won't have twenty-four-seven access to this sweet Boy anymore, but excited because we will be moving on together. I'll be able to take him on public dates, and even to The Grove as my Little. I'll have someone to bitch to about the pitfalls of my job, and he'll also be able to rely on me to help soothe the emotional and physical toll of his job, too.

Accidental and unplanned or not, I wasn't exaggerating when I said that this relationship we're forging really is the best Christmas gift I could have imagined.

I sip a mug of steaming coffee as Anson plays with the toy train, making cute 'choo-choo' sounds as he watches it go around its tiny, circular track. He has put the big snow globe in the middle of the circle and drew himself some paper passengers to ride on the train.

His happiness and excitement are infectious, though I still want to give him a more magical festive experience than this. The plans and ideas I started formulating on Christmas Eve start to solidify in my brain. and I promise myself that I'll make them happen.

For all the joy he has given me over these past couple of days, my unexpected ray of sunshine deserves everything I can imagine and more.

* * *

"Are you sure you're comfortable driving back to the city?" I ask Anson anxiously as I buckle him into the passenger seat of my truck. It feels like we've come full circle in such a short amount of time. But now that we've reached mid-afternoon on the day after Christmas, we finally have to leave our magical Christmas behind for the real world.

He nibbles his bottom lip. "As long as it starts and isn't too damaged from drifting into that tree, yeah."

"Alright, well, I'll be right behind you, okay?" I know he's a grown man, but he's my Boy, and it's understandable if he's shaky after having crashed his car the last time he drove it. When you're not used to driving in sleet and snow, especially with the risk of black ice, it can be a scary experience. "You drive as slow as you need to, and pull over if you need a break, or feel—"

"Daddy," he interrupts me, and the amusement and affection in his tone buoys my spirits, "I'll be fine. I promise. The reports online said they've de-iced the roads, and I know you'll be right behind me if I need you."

I nod. "Okay, fine." Shutting his door, I wander around the truck and climb into the driver's seat, casting one last glance towards the cabin door. "Are you sure you don't need to go potty before—"

"Daddy," he laughs his complaint and shakes his head. "I went, like, five minutes ago. Stop stalling."

"Fine," I grouse, but a smirk tugs at my lips because I know he secretly enjoys me Daddying him, "so sue me if I want to make sure you're comfortable."

"Awww," he teases, reaching across the console to pat my thigh, "are you getting back into your grumpy lumbersnack character now that we're heading home? Because the cranky bear thing is super hot."

"Shut up," I demand, but I can't help grinning. "You're getting bratty, baby."

"Maybe that's 'cause I want my cranky Daddy bear to spank me."

I groan and turn to glare at him. "That's unfair. I'm going to be half hard for the entire drive back now."

"Only half?" He folds his arms and pouts playfully. "I should be worth a full erection, Daddy."

"God, give me strength," I mutter before I put my truck into gear and start the slow, cautious drive down my driveway.

I can hear the smile in Anson's voice when he says, "Viagra works better than prayers. I should know; I'm a doctor."

My laughter echoes around the cab as I drive towards his car, leaving the cabin and our Christmas bubble in the rearview mirror.

Chapter Nineteen – Anson

"So…" Vince corners me in the hospital cafeteria three days after Christmas, sliding his tray onto the table in front of mine as he drops into the seat across from me. His dark eyes glint with curiosity, a little humor, and concern.

It's the same kind of look Drake gave me when we finally parted ways after returning from the mountains, and it makes my heart squeeze with longing.

I push my cafeteria stir-fry around with my plastic spork listlessly. "So?"

"Dude. Are you really going to leave me hanging? How was—" Vince lowers his voice and glances around furtively, as though anyone is going to be listening in over the noise of fifty other conversations, kids crying, and people coughing. "—*everything?*"

I sigh and abandon my meal, not really interested in eating it. After three and a half days of Daddy's cooking, I've been spoiled, and nothing else seems appealing. Vince frowns down at my plate, but I answer him with a despondent, "Incredible."

Distracted by my answer, my best friend smiles and cocks his head. "Yeah? All of it?"

"All of it," I agree, finally smiling at my recent memories. "I'm *so* a Little, Vin. Like…a *little* Little. Like…pacis, diapers, baby-talk…" I breathe in deeply and then let my shoulders sag as I let the air out again. "Drake was —is— amazing. He tried to give me every possible experience I could have wanted in just a few days." Huffing, I slump in my chair and fold my arms, "And all I gave him was a pair of socks that say 'save a horse' on one foot and 'ride a bear' on the other."

Vince snorts and grabs a fry off his plate, biting it in half and waving it around as he says, "Pretty sure you also gave him a weekend of perfect Daddy time, too."

I eye him suspiciously. "That's what he said. Have you talked to him?"

I wouldn't put it past my far-too-protective best friend to follow up on the conversation he'd had with Drake that first night. Sure enough, Vince averts his gaze and shifts in his seat.

"Vin…what did you do?"

"I just wanted to make sure that he was okay, too," he admits, popping another fry into his mouth. "I know we haven't been close or anything, but it wasn't hard to see that he was lonely. And then a few days spent trapped in a cabin with you driving him crazy—"

"Hey!" I protest, but I'm starting to grin now. "I'll have you know, I was the *perfect* Boy. I was on my best behavior."

"So he said," Vince agrees, but he arches an eyebrow at me and then pushes his plate in my direction. I snag a few fries and stuff them into my mouth, much preferring the unhealthy, deep-fried food over the mess of vegetables, rice and oyster sauce on my plate. "You didn't want to be even a little bit bratty? I mean, I know you, man. My money would be on cute brat over angel baby any day of the week."

"I can be both," I insist, snagging a few more fries and munching happily. Through a mouthful, I add, "I like being his good boy, too."

My best friend's mouth twitches underneath his own beard, and complete with the dad bod, I can see far too many similarities between him and Drake. But, I swear, I've never had a thing for Vince. He's my brother from another mother, and even if I sometimes read taboo romance novels, I couldn't ever see my BFF in a romantic or sexual light. *Eww.*

"Yeah, well," Vince says, shaking those disturbing comparisons away, "you should talk to him about exploring your… uh…naughtier side, too. I think he'd enjoy the challenge."

"At the moment, trying to work out when we'll see each other next is challenge enough." And now I'm back to pouting. "Stupid work. I hate it."

"You do not," Vince chides and grabs for his burger. He takes my plastic knife and then butchers his burger into two ragged halves. Taking a bite out of one, he says, "you love your job. The kids are your life."

Yeah, until I have to tell their parents that the results from their bloodwork wasn't promising and that they need to find a pediatric oncologist…

"Sometimes," I reply instead, pushing the pain and sadness from this morning's meeting away. Vince deals with enough trauma in Emergency and doesn't need me piling on top of it. "But right now I wish I was working a normal nine-to-five job so I could make plans to see my boyfriend regularly."

Dark eyebrows drawing down as his eyes line with sympathy, Vince agrees, "Yeah, okay, I get that. Having Bear move in with me made that part a whole lot easier to deal with."

"As fast as my relationship with Drake has developed, I don't think suggesting that we move in after three days together will go down well."

"I don't know…he sounds pretty smitten."

"Smitten?" I blink across the table at him. "Who says 'smitten' these days?"

His cheeks color and he pushes the other half of the burger towards me. "Just shut up and eat."

Chuckling, I do as he says, but his words and the unspoken implication follow me around for the rest of the day. Maybe moving in would be too much, too soon, but who's to say I can't suggest regular alternating sleepovers?

* * *

Stepping into The Little Community Center always makes me smile. Founded by a former cop who is also a lifestyle Daddy, the whole function of this place is to provide support to anyone in the kink community who needs it. They run information sessions, buddy programs, charity auctions, counseling sessions, pro-bono legal assistance and so much more.

The main space is a bright room set up like a giant living room, with couches and beanbags and coffee tables all inviting and welcoming. There are also adult-sized tables and chairs set out with toys and coloring activities, too. Charlie, the founder, and his husband (and Little), Asher, have put a lot of effort into creating an age play friendly space which is not situated in a kink club. It's like a midway point, for people who aren't comfortable going to a club, but who still want to interact with others in the lifestyle.

"Well, hello stranger," Ash greets me as I stride across the main room towards the little reception desk. He gets up from the desk, his mess of floppy curls flying around his face as he shuffles paperwork into a neat pile, then walks out of the little room to greet me properly. "We haven't seen you in ages."

Asher is a true lifestyle Little. He's about my height, if a bit shorter, with what my mother would have called a 'swimmer's build'. He was the first person I met here when I came looking for a bit more personalized information than the internet could provide, and I find his bright, bubbly outlook contagious.

I feel a stab of guilt for not having visited much since I switched over to visiting The Grove once I was ready to properly explore my interest in the lifestyle. I've seen Charlie and Asher at The Grove's Littles' Nights, but it's not quite the same as sitting and talking in a quiet space.

"Sorry," I apologize sheepishly, rubbing the back of my neck.

Asher shakes his head emphatically. "Oh, no, don't be. I get what it's like to be busy with life. Plus, with your job, I'm betting you don't get much downtime." He cocks his head, his hazel eyes sparkling. "So…what brings you back today?"

This is the point where I shrug and squirm a little, because I honestly don't know why I came here. I just felt the pull and went with it.

Allowing my gaze to flit around the main room again, I smile as I take in the Christmas decorations which are still proudly on display. "Need help taking the tree down and getting ready for New Years?" I ask in lieu of answering his question.

"You did not drive halfway across the city just to offer to help me redecorate," he replies and leans against the window to the office. "Especially when you know I have a bevy of Daddies at my beck and call."

"You have one Daddy, little lamb," Charlie's deep, authoritative tone corrects as he steps out from his own office and closes the distance between himself and his husband. He kisses Asher on top of his mop of curls and adds, "and your Uncles spoil you."

Ash just grins at that. "That's 'cause their Littles love me, and they want to keep 'em all happy."

Charlie sighs. "Well, I can't argue with that." He turns his attention to me and smiles, sticking out his hand for me to shake, which I do. "It's good to see you, Anson." His expression morphs into one of sympathy. "I was sorry to hear that things with Tanner didn't work out."

I blink. God, my relationship with Tanner feels like it was eons ago, and not only a month or so. I'd feel guilty for almost forgetting about it, except we were never serious. In fact, whatever feelings I'd had for the cute Little pale in comparison to the deep, intense attachment I've formed for Drake.

"Oh, uh, thanks," I find myself stammering. "But, uh, we're both good. We weren't compatible, and we were better off ending things early than forcing it."

Charlie nods and gestures back towards the main space. "Want a coffee?"

I screw up my nose. "Cocoa?"

"Oooh, great idea!" Asher turns pleading eyes on Charlie. "Please, Daddy?"

"If you spoil your dinner, you're getting corner time."

I watch their conversation with a smile on my face, but it makes my heart squeeze. I miss Drake so badly. He hasn't called me since we've been back in the city. I mean, we've texted a bit, and he arranged to have my car fixed for me, but our schedules have been out of whack, and I know he's been super busy getting back into the swing of running his business. Still, I don't know if I should call him, or if I should give him more time, or—

"You okay?" Asher's question shakes me from my spiraling thoughts and I'm surprised to find that I followed them over to the comfy couches near the coffee station. He tugs me down onto the soft seat of my favorite big, orange couch, and tells Charlie to make my drink, too, silencing my protests when I attempt to say I can do it myself. "Seriously, Anson, what's up? I doubt you came here just to drink all our cocoa."

"I guess…I don't know. I think…I think I wanted to talk to someone?"

I'd been ready to drive my ass over to Drake's bakery to talk about the revelations I'd had at lunch time, but I didn't have a clue what to say to him. Then I'd driven myself here instead.

"I think…I mean, I talked to Vince at lunch, but he's hardly an unbiased third party, so…"

"You're going to have to back up a bit," Charlie interrupts as he hands me a steaming mug of instant cocoa. I sip at it and try not to make a face. It's nowhere near as good as the stuff Drake spoiled me with over Christmas. "What did you want to talk about?"

"Oh!" Ash bounces in his seat beside me, the contents of his own mug sloshing dangerously. "Have you met someone new? Another Little?"

"Your constant matchmaking worries me," Charlie sighs at him, then looks at me expectantly. "But is that it?"

I chuckle before carefully setting my mug down on the table beside the arm of the couch. "I met someone, yeah. Well, I mean, I already knew him." I huff and wonder, momentarily, why I'm so scared to say this out loud. I've already told Vince, and he's the only person whose opinion really matters to me. But these are the guys who basically introduced me to the lifestyle. They answered all of my questions and were right there with me when I said I thought I was a Daddy. My cheeks flame, and I duck my chin to confess, "But he's a Daddy…and I'm, um, not. A Daddy, I mean."

At my side, Asher gasps loudly. "*Really?* Does that mean you're a Boy? A Sub?"

I exhale with a whoosh of relieved air, no longer feeling as panicky now that the truth is out there. "Yeah. A Little, actually." I swallow and glance at Charlie, feeling oddly shy before I smile at Asher. "*So* Little. Like, um, pacis and…*stuff.*"

He thrusts his mug towards his husband and then launches at me, squeezing me in a tight hug. "I'm so happy for you! And, *oh*, Daddy!" He turns to look at Charlie, still not releasing me from his hold, "I get a new friend for playdates!"

"Maybe let him breathe and ask him if he's comfortable with that, first?" Charlie smiles indulgently. Then, while Asher hurries to apologize, says, "Good for you, man. Last time we talked, I got the feeling you hadn't quite *sparked* with the kink…but I take it that's changed?"

Still blushing, I nod. "Yeah. I feel a bit stupid for not realizing that I wasn't a Daddy and that I actually *wanted* a Daddy, but—"

"Nope, we don't use that word," Charlie points his finger at me, his face marred with consternation. "Besides, there's nothing stupid about it at all. The whole Daddy thing was what interested you to begin with, so it makes sense that you started there."

"That's pretty much what Drake said," I sigh.

Asher sits up straighter again. "Drake? Like…*Drake* Drake? The cuddly Daddy who runs the bakery on the corner of

Twelfth Avenue?" He wiggles with excitement. "Is *he* your Daddy? Please say yes! He makes the best cupcakes!"

Is it wrong that I feel a bit jealous that Asher knows what Daddy's cupcakes taste like, but I don't?

Don't answer that.

"Yeah," I start, and Asher squeals. His enthusiasm is infectious, and I find myself grinning despite my moment of childish envy. "We, um, we spent Christmas together, and I accidentally discovered that I'm *really* into being Little—"

Asher squeals again. "This sounds *just* like one of Tony's meet-cute romance novels," he declares, and I have absolutely no idea what he's talking about, but I agree anyway.

"Baby," Charlie sounds exasperated as he looks at his husband, but the look on his face is full of love, "it's great that you're excited for Anson, but you keep interrupting him."

"Sorry," Asher apologizes again, and I shrug.

"It's fine. My thoughts are all jumbled anyway."

He reaches over to squeeze my thigh. "I get it," he nods with understanding, the glimpses of his Little side receding with his seriousness. "When I first realized I was a Little, I really struggled with it. Not that I think you are," he's quick to add, "but even so, it's probably jarring when you thought you were a Daddy. Also," he shrugs, "who's to say you're not, like, an age play Switch or something? A Daddy with some people and a Little with others?"

"Is that a thing?" I ask, frowning as I swivel my gaze between him and Charlie.

Ash pouts a little, lifting his hands up at his sides with their palms up. "I can't see why it can't be."

After considering it for a moment, I decide that it's possible there are people out there who are into playing both roles, but that's not for me. Shaking my head, I admit, "I don't think that's me, though. I found being a Daddy hard. Being Little was…liberating." I think back over the holiday just gone with wistfulness.

I miss Daddy.

Just like that, Asher is back to being his bubbly, bordering-on-Littlespace self. "So, what's the problem? Is it that you think people at The Grove are going to be all 'ugh, weren't you a Daddy?' or something?"

That concern never even crossed my mind. "No…it's just…I guess I miss Daddy. A lot. Only I haven't really spoken to him since the day after Christmas and, I mean, we did kind of fall into a super serious relationship really fast and…I don't know. I just…I wanted to talk it out with an unbiased party before I turned up on his doorstep demanding cuddles and a paci."

Or to fuck him and claim him as mine.

So sue me, I've been watching a lot of porn since I've been left to my own devices. But it's not just about the sex or the kink.

"And it's not that I don't think he'd like that," I hurry to add, "because we talked about everything, and I think we're on the same page. I mean, I know he cares because he's been texting, and he got some guy to fix my car, so I'm not, like, afraid that he's changed his mind or anything. But…sometimes I don't trust my own impulses, y'know?"

And there's my lightbulb moment of the day. *That's* the reason I came here instead of tracking Drake down. I trust him wholeheartedly to have been completely honest with me and, especially after talking to Vince, I know he would be happy to see me. But I'm still unsure that I can trust my instincts now, when until this point they were leading me down the wrong path.

Like…what if I'm not really a Little after all and I've just led Drake on? I would hate myself for hurting him.

"So, you're questioning whether you're really a Little?" Charlie puts my garbled thoughts into a succinct question.

I bob my head so quickly my teeth clack together. Scooting to the edge of my seat, I clasp my hands tightly between my spread knees and lean forward. "If I was wrong about being a Daddy…"

"You said being Little was liberating," he takes over calmly. I find his low, gravelly voice soothing. He's very Daddy. Just not *my* Daddy. "Why?"

I blink. "Why what?"

"Why did it feel liberating? You chose that word for a reason. You didn't say it felt sexy, or kinky, or naughty. You said 'liberating'. Why?"

"Well…because it felt…it felt…" Like I could finally let go and just be myself. Like I didn't have to put on a role to make someone else happy, or to keep someone else calm. Like I didn't have to worry about anything other than just enjoying myself. Hell, I didn't even really have to worry about going to the bathroom! I could just be free of any and all concerns or stresses.

And there goes *another* lightbulb.

"Oh," I finish lamely.

Charlie's right: my primary motivation to stay Little wasn't the kink. It wasn't the sex, even though I *really* enjoy the sex. It wasn't that I was trying to fit a mold or play a role. It was that being Little comes naturally to me.

Being with Drake comes naturally to me.

Charlie grins knowingly at me. "So, are you still worried

that you can't trust your gut on this one?"

I turn to Asher, a rush of joy bringing my own Little side forward as I ask, "Can I hug your Daddy?"

Asher beams back at me. "He's the best, right?"

My thoughts drift to Drake and I only *just* manage not to refute his claim.

Charlie snorts, though, and I'm pretty sure he knows what I was thinking. Still, I give him a hug and thank them both for letting me talk out the antsy feeling that I hadn't been able to shake.

Now to find my Daddy...

...and claim him.

Chapter Twenty – Drake

"Hello?" I answer my phone distractedly, not even bothering to look at the caller ID.

Leaving the bakery to my two very competent staff members over the holiday —only closing it for Christmas Day— has left me with a pile of paperwork to complete. I've spent the past couple of days going back over their inventory notes, double checking that they have followed all the health and safety regulations for the food products stored on site, and placing some emergency orders with our suppliers…all between running the bakery single-handedly while they took their well-earned time off.

Sadly, all of that has left me with very little time to think of anything outside of managing my business. I even accidentally slept here the other night, waking up at my desk disoriented and with a pain in my neck.

The time off was definitely worth it, especially when I think about Anson, but I need to get caught up if I want any chance of putting my plans to fix his Christmas experience into action.

"Daddy?" Anson's voice on the other end of the call gets my complete attention. My heart speeds up and my lips pull into an involuntary, but no less genuine, smile.

"Hey, sunshine, how are you?" I lean back in my office chair, stifling a groan at the kinks in my neck and back.

"Better now that I've heard your voice again," he answers.

Immediately, I feel guilty for not having reached out. I made sure to have his car looked over so I could rest easy knowing that he was safe to drive it, I've sent a handful of texts to let him know I was thinking about him, but I know better than that.

I'm out of practice as a Daddy, and it's showing.

"I'm so sorry, baby. I should have called. I've been drowning with work stuff…not that that's any excuse. But—"

"It's fine, Daddy. We're both adults, and this is very new so it's out of routine to call each other. Not to mention, I can only imagine how hard it is to run your own business. Plus, you did warn me that you were working on your own this week." There's a pause before he says, "I hope you're taking care of yourself, too."

It takes me a moment to process the stream-of-consciousness-style reply. Over the holiday, I did notice that Anson tends to get wordy when he's anxious, so I still feel bad for not prioritizing a proper check-in with him. Even if he's not upset, he deserved at least that from me.

I will do better.

"I'm feeling better for hearing your voice, too," I admit, neatly sidestepping his suggestion that I might not be taking the best care of myself. "I really miss you."

"I miss you, too." I might be imagining it, but I'm pretty sure I hear relief in his voice. "I know you're busy, but, um, can I see you? I can just sit in a corner with a book or something while you work. I just…well, I really want to see you, is all."

I couldn't deny him even if I wanted to. Looking over my desk, with its mess of papers, dirty coffee mug and no less than three empty energy drink cans, I decide this mess can wait until tomorrow morning.

"Of course, baby. I'm still at the bakery right now, but—"

"Oh, good," he cuts me off with a relieved sigh, "because I just parked outside."

My sweet, impulsive Boy, I think with a shake of my head. Grinning, I say, "I'll be right out to let you in." Then I end the call and push my rolling chair back.

My "office" is barely more than a storage cupboard behind the kitchen. I stride through the kitchen itself, double checking that everything is still gleaming and spotless from my closing clean, and then into the small, rectangular retail space. I glance around here, too, making sure the counters are still clean and that the display cases are all empty. The only light at the moment is coming from the soda fridge against the far wall, the lines of bottles and cans inside backlit by glowing white LEDs.

Letting myself around the counter, I make it to the front door, which I closed and locked hours ago, and feel some of the remaining tension in my shoulders melt away when I come face to face with Anson's sheepish smile through the glass.

Within seconds of unlocking the door, he's in my arms, kissing me in greeting.

God, I've missed him.

I kiss him back, and we lose ourselves in the simple act of reconnecting until the need for air overrides the need to feel his tongue in my mouth.

"Hey," I greet him after I've pulled away, my voice a bit more gravelly for the enthusiastic hello.

"Hi, Daddy," he nibbles his bottom lip. "I'm sorry I just turned up here. I know I should have checked—"

"I love visits from my sexy boyfriend," I tell him before he can work himself up into another ramble. "You can surprise me any time. But double checking if I'm here or at home is probably also a good idea."

"Mmm," he sighs happily, "I love it when you call me that."

"What? Sexy?"

"Your boyfriend."

The way he says it is so cute, I can't resist kissing the tip of his nose. "Well, that's what we agreed to be for each other, right?"

"Uh-huh," he's starting to sound more like his Little self, "but I like hearing it."

The bakery is not an appropriate space to indulge his regression, and once again I want to slap myself for not considering how badly he might need to slip back into Littlespace after spending three full days immersed in it.

"Are you feeling Big enough to drive?" I ask him, pulling my keys from my pocket as I start turning off lights and move to set the alarm for the night. "Because I think we should go back to my place. It's about twenty minutes away." With the alarm going into its thirty-second countdown to being armed, I usher Anson through the front door and, with us both outside in the cool night air, turn back to lock it. "It's okay if you're not: we can leave your car here and I can bring you back later to pick it up."

"Nah, I'm good to drive. Um," he clears his throat, "can I…I mean, it's presumptuous of me, but I've got an overnight bag which I keep in my car for all-nighters at the hospital, if…y'know…it's okay for me to stay the night with you."

"I want that more than anything. But you're okay with me getting up at, like, three a.m.? I'm usually in the store by four. You don't have to leave that early," I rush to assure him, "I'll leave you a spare key so you can lock up. But—"

"You trust me with a key to your house?" Anson's blue eyes have gone wide. "Daddy, that's…that's *huge*."

"Baby," I step in closer to him, holding his biceps while I look him in the eye, needing him to hear the truth in my explanation, "you trust me with so much more than that every time you regress. I'm happy for you to keep the key and let yourself in anytime you want. Day or night, I want my home to be a safe space for you, whether I'm there or not."

He chews on his bottom lip again before he wraps me in a huge, tight hug. "You're the best Daddy ever."

My heart squeezes at the adoration in his words.

"I'm not," I tell him with a touch of self-deprecation as I pull back. "I dropped the ball this week. But I'm going to do better, and the key thing? It's just the beginning of that. Now," I add when it looks like he's going to argue, "let's get going, hmm? Have you eaten?"

* * *

If I'd thought sharing my cabin with Anson had felt right, the feeling has nothing on how amazing it is to have him in my home. I tell him to treat it like his own home. I don't want him behaving like a guest here: I want him to be my equal in this space.

After feeding him a light dinner, he shyly asked if he could be Little for a while and I leapt at the chance to reconnect as Daddy and Boy. I dressed him in a diaper and footed pajamas —the pants covered in cartoon monster trucks and the long-sleeved shirt emblazoned with a matching picture and the words 'I Drive Daddy Crazy'— and now we're snuggled up on the couch, with him reclined in my arms so I can give him his bottle of warm milk. There's a Disney movie playing on the TV, but neither of us are really watching it. We're watching each other, instead.

It's only been a few days since we last indulged our need for this kind of play, but it's obvious to me, at least,that we needed it.

"Daddy," he starts softly when I set aside his now-empty bottle, "I like your house. It's big…an'…friendly."

It's a standard family ranch-style home. Brick and tile, four bedrooms, two bathrooms, and a generous backyard. But I've worked hard to modernize it, and to make it feel like somewhere I want to spend my downtime. I've converted one of the spare bedrooms into my home office, and another as a nursery-slash-playroom, and the rest of the house has been repainted in bright white with even brighter accent colors. The living room, where we are now, has a bright green feature wall, and the kitchen to our right has a matching bright green backsplash behind the stovetop.

My furniture is all worn and scuffed, and the walls are home to art prints and photos. My home looks and feels lived-in, but it makes me happy to hear that it feels 'friendly' to my Boy.

"I'm glad, sunshine. Did you like the playroom?"

He grins. "There's a big train set."

"There is."

"An' a big box of blocks."

"Yep."

"An' a special table for diaper changes." He wriggles his butt. "That made me feel extra Little."

I'd splurged on having the custom piece of furniture made for that reason. It adds an additional element to the role play which I've enjoyed over the years, and I'm glad that Anson feels it, too.

"I'm happy to hear that, sweetheart."

There's also a twin bed in the room as well, but it's never been used for nap times or overnight stays. It really just seems to exist as a place to display the mountain of stuffies who also live in the playroom.

"But my favorite part of your house is your room, Daddy."

"Oh?"

"Yeah. 'Cause the bed is big an' soft, an' the window looks out at the trees, an' also 'cause it's where you sleep."

Trying to hide my amusement, I ask, "Is that a hint, sunshine? Do you want to go to bed?"

The lip nibbling starts again, and his expression turns coy. "Not yet, Daddy. Maybe…maybe after I get changed and Big again?"

That is new. Our routine in the cabin always saw him going to bed Little. Not that I mind, either way.

"Do you want to be Big before bed? Because you know I'm happy for you to stay Little for as long as you want."

"I know…but, Daddy," he sits up, looking absolutely adorable as he puts on his 'serious' face, "I wanna be Big with you, too. I wanna be all the ways with you."

I melt for him like I always do. He's too perfect not to fall head over heels for. We might barely have been together for long, but I'm pretty sure I'm in love with him at this point.

"I want to be all the ways with you, too. But we don't have to do it all at once. We're not going to turn back into rats and pumpkins after midnight."

Anson rolls his eyes but a smile lifts his lips. "You're silly, Daddy. I just...I want *everything* with you."

The words might not be the same as the three that are dancing on the tip of my tongue, but I hear them nonetheless. "You'll get it, baby, I promise."

* * *

"Drake?"

The sound of my name tugs me out of dreamland. "Hmm?"

"You awake?"

"I am now," I grumble gently, squinting into the darkness.

"Good. I couldn't sleep," he adds softly. "I've missed you, and I watched a *lot* of porn over the last few days and...I just...*I need you.*"

I barely have a moment for my sluggish, sleepy brain to process that before I'm being pushed onto my back and Anson's mouth is trailing a wet, warm path down my hairy chest and belly. And, *oh God*, down to my cock.

I gasp and fist the sheets. "Baby, what—?"

I have no idea what time it is. We went to bed around nine, with Anson remaining Little after I reassured him that I'm happy to spend time with him in any headspace, and I fell asleep listening to his measured breathing and warm puffs of his breath against my chest.

Being woken up by a completely different version of my boyfriend is not something I'll complain about, but it is wildly disorienting...especially when I feel him pull down my sleep pants and take my rapidly hardening shaft all the way into his mouth.

"Holy fuck," I groan, closing my eyes as the pleasure registers in my brain. "*Anson…*"

He moans, and I feel the sound vibrate through my shaft and directly to my balls.

"Oh, God…"

He sucks my cock like its his favorite flavored popsicle, bobbing his head up and down my length while I do everything in my power not to fuck up into the delicious wet heat of his mouth. Then, just as my balls draw up and I'm certain I'm going to come, he pulls off with a *pop* of released suction.

"You fucking tease," I accuse, weakly lifting my head to glare down in his direction.

The room is still dark, but I can just make out Anson's features in what little light is making its way past the black-out curtains covering the window. He seems very self-satisfied.

"I'm just getting the lube," he tells me before the mattress dips with his movement.

"Baby," I whine at him, though I don't make any attempt to stop him from reaching my bedroom drawer, "I can't—I mean, if I try to fuck you now, I'll come within seconds."

He chuckles, locates the (admittedly large) bottle in question, then settles himself between my legs again. The smirk on his face is salacious and it makes my dick twitch with additional interest. "Who said anything about *you* fucking *me*?"

Chapter Twenty-One — Anson

For half a second, I'm afraid I've been presumptuous and impulsive again. Knowing that Drake is vers like I apparently am now doesn't necessarily mean that I can just assume he's okay with me fucking him right now. But the way he throws his head back and groans *"Fuuuuck"* long and low tells me he's okay with my plan.

I'm very glad that he is. I wasn't lying when I said I've watched a lot of porn, and as much as I've learned that I do enjoy bottoming, I've missed topping. Plus, despite how obviously busy Drake has been, he still managed to arrange for my car's minor repairs after we got back to the city. Apparently, one of his regular customers is a mechanic or auto-electrician or whatever. Either way, even though we didn't get a chance to talk outside of texting, Drake still arranged that for me: something I didn't properly thank him for.

Yeah, we both dropped the ball by not communicating properly these past few days, but he still proved that he was my perfect, amazing Daddy by taking that adult stress off my plate. I just want to take care of him my way in return. I want him to feel worshiped and claimed the same way he makes me feel.

Naturally, because of the way my brain works, these thoughts whirred around and around in my head as I stared into the darkness until the desperation to act on the impulses finally got to me.

Thank God he's happy to be woken up in the middle of the night for sex, right?

I've definitely found the perfect man for me.

It's not long before I have two lubed fingers thrusting in and out of him while he babbles and begs for my cock, and the thrill of seeing this big, brawny man spread out for me is intense.

Mine, my brain cheers. *All mine.*

"You ready for me?" I ask, smirking when he nods so fast I think he might just give himself whiplash.

"Please, baby. *Now*. I need you in me."

You hear that? My Daddy is *begging* me to fuck him. It's music to my ears.

I withdraw my fingers to slick myself up, and then I move forward, pulling his thick, hairy legs up over my shoulders as I sink inside him. We make matching sounds of pleasure, but I'm careful not to go too fast. I know it's been a while for him —though the almost intimidating size of the toy in his drawer suggests he can take me without any issues at all— and I had him on the edge of coming from my blowjob before, too.

"You feel so good," he mutters, rocking his hips. "Fuck, Anson, baby…*move*. I need you to move. Faster. Harder."

I snort, but start moving as instructed. I want him to enjoy this, after all. I want to know how he likes it and deliver that. Even so, it doesn't stop me from teasing, "You're a very bossy bottom, you know that?"

"I'm still —oh, fuck, *right there*— a Daddy, sunshine."

"You are," I start to pant as my pace picks up and I try to find the angle that made his breath catch just now, "Y-you're *my* Daddy."

Mine.

"Yes," he says emphatically, the 's' turning into a sibilant hiss, and I don't know if he's agreeing with me, or if I nailed his prostate again, "keep…*nnngh*…keep doing that for Daddy."

I'm nowhere near Littlespace right now, but I love hearing him talk like that. The fact that he's still in Daddy-mode, even while I'm nailing him, is just so *him*.

"Are you going to come for me, Daddy?" I ask him between heavy breaths. My fingers dig into his thighs where I'm holding onto them over my chest. Despite the coolness of the winter air, I feel sweaty and slippery. My hair is flopping over my eyes, and I don't have the mental or physical capacity to brush it aside. "Am I being a good boy for you?"

"Anson…Anson…fuck," Drake releases the twisted hold he had on the sheets and wraps one of his fists around his cock. He starts jerking himself while I practically pound into him, our bodies making a rhythmic, fleshy *slap, slap, slap* sound with every completed thrust. "Harder. Fuck me…harder…God, yes, just like that. Oh! Fuck! *There*! There, Anson, *fuck*…"

"T-tell me I'm being a good b-boy, Daddy," I demand, obsessed with the way he's unraveling on my cock.

Mine, I think with a primal sort of energy, my brain echoing the word with every slam of my body into his. *Mine. Mine. Mine.*

I've always enjoyed sex, but this? This is something else. It feels bigger, somehow. Powerful. More intense.

This stolen moment when we both should have been sleeping, knowing that work is just around the corner for us, was something I had to have. Drake's tight ass clenching around my bare cock is something I had to have. Watching him lose himself in the pleasure I'm providing is something I had to have.

"I'm going to come," he warns, ignoring my words. "Baby, I'm going to come."

"Tell me, Daddy," I insist with an almost feral intensity. "Tell me I'm—"

"Fuck, baby, you're a good boy," he cuts me off, almost crying the praise, "you're *my* good boy. The best b—*oh*, fuck, I'm coming. I...*unngh.*"

I wish I'd thought to turn the lights on to watch him make a mess over his hand and belly as he lets out that sexy, guttural sound. But the feeling of him squeezing around me as his body locks up during orgasm is too much for me to handle, and then I'm coming, too, filling him up in waves of bliss that are over far too soon.

I wish I'd turned the lights on so I could watch my cum dribbling out of him, too.

We collapse in a sweaty, cum-streaked mess once I've pulled out of him, both of us breathing heavily. Drake kisses the top of my head and I hum happily, snuggling into him as I enjoy the last of the afterglow, my weird possessive energy fading away to a dull, satisfied thrum at the back of my brain.

One sexy Daddy successfully claimed.

Just as the silence between us drifts on a touch too long and I think he's fallen asleep, he asks, "Have I mentioned how much I love your impulsiveness?"

Where most people —my best friend included— find that

part of me frustrating, the fact that Drake not only rolls with it but says that he loves it makes me feel oddly emotional.

Swallowing thickly, I narrowly avoid blurting out that I just love him in general, because even my impulsive ass knows it's too soon for that. Instead, I manage, "I'm glad," but that's all I can think to say. After a beat I force myself to sit up. "I'll go get a cloth to clean us up."

Drake groans and rolls over, reaching for his phone on the nightstand. He taps the screen and we both flinch when it lights up.

"It's almost three," he says, clicking the side button to sleep the screen again, "I've got to get up anyway. Shower with me?"

"I'll never say no to an offer like that."

* * *

"Hottie at three o'clock," my colleague, Annabelle, leans in to tell me, her eyes glinting with humor.

I volunteered to pick up an additional evening shift in Emergency tonight, knowing that it will be a busy one. New Year's Eve always is, and I was lucky enough to be rostered off for Christmas, so working extra tonight only seems fair. I texted Daddy earlier to let him know that I'll be a few hours late getting back to his place, but we can still ring in the New Year together.

Annabelle's gaze shifts over my left shoulder and she winks brazenly at whatever specimen has caught her attention. It makes me laugh, because she really is like the female version of me, complete with blue eyes and blonde hair. We have been mistaken for siblings before.

"Hello, handsome," the flirty words don't come from

Annabelle, though. They come from directly behind me, issued in a low, husky voice that I'd be able to recognize anywhere by now.

I can feel my expression go slack with surprise before I spin around on the spot. Sure enough, Drake is standing right there.

"Da—Drake!" I cry with joy, catching my near-slip just in time. "What are you doing here?" I look him over for any signs of injury. "Did you hurt yourself at work?" God knows there are a million ways he could do some damage inside a bakery.

He chuckles and shakes his head. "Social visit only," he answers, dipping his chin in Annabelle's direction. "Hi."

She sidles up beside me, not even pretending to hide her curiosity. "Where on earth have you been hiding this one, Anson? It seems cruel that you haven't shared." She offers Drake her hand. "I'm Annabelle, Anson's favorite colleague."

Drake shoots me a knowing look as he takes her hand and shakes it. "Drake Connors. It's a pleasure. I'm sure the two of you keep your superiors on their toes."

"I'll have you know we tone it down around the patients," I huff defensively. "We can be professional."

Benji, one of the orderlies, must overhear me as he passes by because he snorts. "Whoever put the two of you on shift together again is a moron," he adds his two cents' worth, then does a double take as he eyes Drake.

"*Hello*, Daddy," he croons, making Drake startle as I growl possessively and Annabelle bursts into peals of laughter. Benji steps away from the empty hospital bed he had been pushing down the corridor and juts out his hip, making no secret of his interest in *my* boyfriend. He sticks out his hand. "I'm Benji," he says, following it up with, "please tell me you have a twin brother."

"I do not," Drake shakes his hand, "but if you're really looking for a Daddy, I can point you towards a great club." He looks Benji over and smirks. "I know a number of men who would enjoy spanking that sass out of you."

Annabelle chokes and it's my turn to chortle as Benji blushes bright red. Who knew my Daddy could be so snarky?

"Oh, Annie," Benji leans against me, even while I cringe at the awful nickname he insists on using for me, "I'm so jealous. He's perfect."

"Uh-huh," I agree, pushing him back towards his abandoned bed, "and he's mine. Find your own."

"I want the name of that club," is all he says before he gets back to his job and somehow manages to saunter away while still pushing the bed.

Annabelle squeezes my bicep. "I'll go see the next patient and give you a minute to catch up." She smiles at Drake. "It really was lovely meeting you. Take care of this one," she bumps my shoulder with hers, "okay? And don't mind Benji; he's all bark, no bite."

"I know how to handle brats like him," Drake says, and I try not to pout because I'm the only brat he should be handling.

Annabelle nudges me again. "I'll buy you five minutes. But you owe me."

"I'll get the next round of coffees," I tell her and she's satisfied with that response.

Once she's gone, Drake says, "Your colleagues are… interesting."

"Benji's getting his own damn Daddy," I blurt petulantly. "You're *mine*."

He laughs and pulls me into a hug, kissing the top of my head. "You're the only impulsive, sassy, naughty Boy I want, sunshine, I promise."

"M'not naughty," I continue to pout, even though his words make me feel all warm and gooey inside.

"Oh, I know there's a bratty side to you, baby. Just because I haven't met it yet, doesn't mean I don't know it's there. You are *far* too feisty and spontaneous for there not to be." He shifts so he can nuzzle my cheek with his bushy, bearded one, then whispers in my ear, "And I can't wait until you give me a reason to spank you."

I gasp and squirm, not wanting to get hard in my scrubs. They won't do a damn thing to hide an erection. *"Daddy,"* I hiss, "that's not playing fair."

"No, seeing you all dressed up in your sexy doctor's getup isn't playing fair. The lab coat is doing it for me."

I can't resist lowering my tone to suggest: "Maybe we can play doctor later."

His cheeks turn pink.

I am definitely taking my lab coat home with me.

"Anyway, I just wanted to come by and make sure you didn't need anything, seeing as you won't be, uh, getting off until late. No pun intended."

Groaning, I laugh. "Leave the dirty jokes for me. But," I consider the sweet gesture, "um, maybe you could swing by my place and get some extra clothes —Big and Little— from my closet?" I fish my house keys out of my pocket and hand them to him. "I'd like to stay a couple of extra nights at your house, if that's okay? I've missed you."

Drake snags the keys from my grasp and swoops in to give me a quick kiss. "That's more than okay, baby. I miss you when you're not there, too."

We've talked every day since the night I stayed over at

his place, but we're still working out a routine around our opposing work schedules. Just seeing him now, even though it's only a short visit at work, has relaxed me in ways I can't fully articulate. I understand now, more than ever, why Vince moved Bear into his house after only a couple of months of dating. If I could move in with my Daddy now, after only a week together, I would do it without hesitation.

But neither of us are ready to make that suggestion out loud, so I'll settle for staying over for a few consecutive nights instead.

"Doctor Meyers," Brenda, one of the nurses, approaches me with a clipboard clutched to her chest. She looks harried. "We've just had an influx of teenagers with suspected alcohol poisoning…"

Drake's expression turns somber, and he steps back. "That sounds serious. I'll let you get back to work." He holds up my keys, letting them jangle a little, "I'll get your stuff and see you at my place later."

My attention is already on the kids coming in, but I nod and offer him an appreciative smile. "Thanks. I'll see you soon. Love you."

It's not until much later, after I've turned on my heel and have swiftly made my way to the first fifteen-year-old passed out on a stretcher, that I realize what I said.

Well, fuck.

Chapter Twenty-Two – Drake

Did he just...?
As Anson rushes away to save some kids' lives, his words repeat in my head. I don't know how long I stand there in that hospital hallway, struck dumb with my heart pounding.

The sweet dismissal was a reflex, I know, but it doesn't make the words feel any less real.

'I love you, too.' I think, far too late to actually reply.

I want to tell him. I want to race after him, pull him into my arms like some cheesy Hollywood montage, with orchestral music building to a crescendo before I declare my feelings and then kiss him within an inch of his life.

But, for obvious reasons, I don't do that.

What I do instead is force one foot in front of the other until I'm back in my car, then I concentrate on getting home, knowing I have work to do.

I spend hours decorating my living room. This is something I've been planning for the past week, and I'll be damned if I cut corners or give my Boy anything less than the perfect vision in my head.

I lug boxes around, string lights along the ceiling, and lay out the gifts I've bought since Christmas. Yes, it's New Year's Eve, but I don't think a few days' delay is going to worry my Boy at all. Especially when he's got no idea any of this is coming.

I'm surveying my handiwork when Anson texts to let me know he's heading my way. The clothes I picked up from his apartment are already hanging in my closet and folded in the drawer I cleared out for him, and I realize I've got less than half an hour before he'll be here.

Equal parts nervous and excited, I make my way into the shower to wash off the sweat and grime from my evening activities. I trim my beard and style my hair with gel, splashing on cologne just as I hear his car pull into my driveway.

Hastily tugging on the Henley I spent far too long picking out, I rush down my short hallway to greet him at the front door, turning off the lights along the way. Glancing into the living room, the fairy-lights I strung up twinkle merrily in the darkness, giving the space a magical ambiance.

"Hey," Anson says awkwardly, stepping through the front door. He nibbles his lower lip and looks at the tiled floor. "Um, about earlier—"

"Wait." I interrupt, causing him to whip his head up to look at me. I reach for his hand, and he takes it, easing some of my anxiety. "Come with me."

The hallway opens up with a large archway on the left, leading to my carpeted living room. I glance around again as Anson gasps and squeezes my hand, and I wait with bated breath to hear what he thinks.

The ceiling is strung with rows of twinkling lights, and so is the large, decorated pine tree in the bay window which looks out to the street. My driveway is on the other side of the house, so I doubt Anson would have seen the display as he walked to the front door.

I've gone all out with my festive decorations, from the lush tree, to the large train set circling it, to the statues of reindeer and snowmen, also lit from within by LEDs. There are also beautifully wrapped boxes containing presents for Anson, and there's a checkered picnic rug spread out on the floor, where the couch has been pushed aside, with an epic charcuterie platter and goblets of mulled wine.

"Drake..." Anson takes it all in and I can't tear my gaze away, watching as the emotions play out over his handsome face. "This is beautiful."

"Merry Christmas, sunshine," I murmur. "I wanted to give you the holiday you deserved."

He turns to look at me, shaking his head. "Christmas was a week ago, and it was perfect! You didn't have to do this."

"I wanted to," I insist. "I want us to always remember our first Christmas together as something truly special."

Those wide, blue eyes of his alight on the small pile of presents and he frowns. "But...I still don't have anything for you."

I recall the time in the cabin. The feeling of embracing being a Daddy again. Being given his trust and seeing him at his most vulnerable. Being the first man in a decade to sink inside him. Being told that he wants a relationship with me.

Then earlier tonight, when he was so genuinely overjoyed to see me at the hospital. His adorable possessive streak when that other guy flirted with me. The sweet, impulsive, reflexive way he told me he loved me...

"You said that you love me," I answer softly, hoping that my tone truly conveys the awe and warmth that the memory inspires inside me. "Baby, there's nothing more in this world you could give me that could possibly top that. And I know it just slipped out and you weren't thinking," I add with a light chuckle when he cringes, and I bring his hand up to my lips so I can brush a kiss to the backs of his knuckles, "but you still said it, and it made my entire year."

"Daddy…" his eyes are shining with more than just the reflection from the lights, and his voice wobbles.

"I suck with words sometimes, Anson," I continue, then I use the hand not holding his to gesture around the room, "but this is hopefully my way of showing you that I feel the same way." My heart thuds in my chest so heavily and rapidly that I'm convinced he can hear it. Steeling myself, I take a deep breath and finish, "I love you, too."

There's a brief, terrifying moment where I'm afraid he's going to tell me that his reflexive farewell earlier was a mistake, but a heartbeat later, his arms are around me and he's kissing me deeply. Relief and arousal shuttle through me, my hands traversing his firm back and shoulders, kneading his ass, wanting to touch every bit of him that I can reach so I can reassure myself that this whole surreal night —*week*, even— has been real.

When we finally part, his lips are reddened and spit-slicked, the skin around his mouth also rubbed a little raw from my beard. I have the urge to mark him all over, to lay my physical claim on him so everyone knows that he's mine and only mine.

"Come on, let's sit and drink the wine before it gets too cold," I tell him, fighting against the primal urge to drag him to my bedroom. I set this night up for him: it shouldn't go to waste.

Anson takes the room in again and then, biting his lip, looks up at me from beneath his lashes. "Can I…um…" I wait for him to finish the thought, but he shakes his head. "Never mind. It's dumb,"

"Nope." Gently reaching out to hold his chin between my index finger and thumb, I look him in the eye. "Ask. This is a safe space, remember? Nothing is silly, or dumb, or off-limits. If I'm not comfortable, I will say so, and we can go from there if that's the case. Okay?"

He swallows, then nods shortly in my careful hold. "Yes, Daddy."

Trying not to let the sweet and still somehow incredibly sexy way he's answered derail the conversation, I let go of his chin and prompt. "So. Can you…?"

"I want to sit in your lap while we eat."

I blink. There's nothing strange about the request. Just as I'm about to say as much, he sighs.

"I mean…like…I want us to be naked. And I want to sit…um…sit on your cock. While we eat."

Holy fuck.

My brain short-circuits.

Anson takes my stunned silence in the worst possible way and blushes, stepping backwards, "See? I told you it was dumb. I don't even know where that came from. Too much porn maybe? Just…just forget—"

"Nope." I interrupt him, reaching out so he can't pull back too far. I grab his hand and squeeze it as I look him in the eye. "That came from somewhere. Is it something you really want? Because it's hot as fuck, but until Christmas, you hadn't even bottomed…"

"I really have been watching a lot of porn," he repeats, but I know that can't be it. "And, um, I've always enjoyed watching cockwarming scenes. They just…they look so much more intimate, you know? Because it's not about the race to the finish line or whatever."

"True, but sometimes it's about control, and I might be your Daddy, honey, but I'm not into power plays."

"Yeah, no, I don't want that. I just…" his cheeks turn bright red again.

"You just what?"

"I want you to be a part of me." He scrunches his nose and looks away. "*Ugh*. That sounds so stupid out loud."

My heart squeezes. "Hey, no. Look at me." With burning cheeks, he does as he's asked and I smile at him. "It doesn't sound stupid. I like the idea of being connected like that, too. You're right: it can be intimate and special. I feel privileged that you want to do that with me."

"Really?"

"Uh-huh."

"And you don't think it's ridiculous? Because—"

"Strip," I interrupt him, tugging my Henley over my head, figuring the best way to show him how serious I am is to follow through with actions. "Now."

"You really don't have to—"

"Anson, that was an order. Don't make me spank you."

The surprise on his face melts into contemplation, a naughty gleam overcoming those pretty blue eyes of his. "Maybe I'd like a spanking."

I groan. "Now is not the time to show me your bratty side, sunshine. Not when you've gotten me so hard it hurts." I reach out and grab his wrist, guiding his hand over my crotch so he can feel the corroborating evidence of my claim. "Now, strip."

"Yes, Daddy," he repeats, and there's still a hint of that temptation to try me in his tone.

I swat his ass hard enough to make him yelp. "That's a taste of what you'll get if you're naughty, baby."

He rubs the sore spot and nods. "Message received. Cock warming and food first, bratty play later."

I snort, but my reply dies on the tip of my tongue as he deftly undresses, leaving his clothes in a puddle of fabric on the floor. When we're both naked, our excitement is more than obvious, and it takes all my self-control while I'm kissing and stretching him out to not just fuck him right here in the middle of my 'Christmas 2.0' display.

"I-I'm good, Daddy," he stammers. "Sit on the picnic rug. I'm hungry."

"What happened to bratty play later, hmm?" I ask with amusement, despite moving over to the rug and sitting cross-legged in front of the tray of food.

Anson crawls over with a cheeky grin and kisses me on the lips before he turns away, kneeling with his back to me. It takes some maneuvering, but it's not long before he's slowly sinking down on my aching cock, making us both moan.

The urge to thrust is overwhelming.

"Y-you good?" I ask him once he's properly seated, our flesh pressed tightly together.

It seems unbelievable to me that a week ago, he considered himself a top and now he's suggested something like this. Something so intimate and deliciously torturous for us both.

"Uh-huh," he exhales. "So full. But…fuck, Daddy, I just love having you inside me. I want you to live there."

The heat and clench of him is incredible. "I'd never get anything done if I did," I reply honestly and he laughs, which makes him bounce a little on my dick. The sensation is stupidly pleasurable, and I groan. "Fuck. I might just come like this, baby."

He cranes his neck to glare at me over his shoulder. "Don't you dare. Not yet. We haven't even eaten anything yet."

I groan some more as he leans forward to collect bits of cheese and cured meats from the platter in front of us, carefully twisting once he's upright so he can offer me a tasty morsel of food over the smooth expanse of his shoulder. I nip at the tips of his fingers as I take the bite from him, barely tasting the burst of salt and umami over the rush of affection and adrenaline his actions have set off inside me.

"My turn, Daddy," he demands, and it takes me another half a second to understand that he's grabbed my hand and is putting a cracker with some selection of cheese and meat into it. "Feed me."

I grin, loving this brazen, cheeky side of him, and I lift the food up, straightening my back so I can attempt to see what I'm doing.

He moans, and I don't know if it's at the taste of the food that he's just taken from me, or at the accidental movement of my cock when I straightened up.

"More, Daddy," he insists, moving his hips in a slow grind, "I need more."

"More food?" At this point, I'd give him more of anything he asked for.

"Mmmhmm."

I try to bite back my own moan as he leans forward again to layer another cracker with meat and cheese, and I'm definitely breathing heavier as he places it between my waiting fingers and thumb. I bring the food to his mouth and this time he licks at my digits as he takes the bite from them.

Swallowing roughly, I ask for my wine.

The scent of cinnamon and cloves wafts to my nose as I take the goblet from him and raise it to my lips. It's barely lukewarm now, but the fragrant red wine is sweet and decadent as I sip at it, trying to moisten my dry throat.

Anson sips at his own, too.

"Wow," he declares, setting his goblet back down on the tray, "that's really nice. I've never had mulled wine before."

"I made it myself. Well," I relent at the arched eyebrow he casts over his shoulder, "I took two bottles of already great merlot and added some spices and sugar and put it all in the crock pot." I press a kiss to the back of his neck. "I'm glad you like it."

It would have been even more enjoyable at the cabin, with the snow falling and the fire crackling, but this way is nice, too. Especially with him warming my cock so beautifully as we enjoy the spread of goodies I organized.

"I'm a pretty crappy cook myself," he admits, lifting a gooey slice of brie on a thin wafer cracker for me to take from his long, elegant fingers. "I mostly eat takeout or microwave meals."

I can't help cringing at that. "You need to take better care of yourself, sunshine."

"It's usually healthy takeout," he replies defensively, then turns his nose up. "I *am* a doctor, Daddy."

Why do I love his petulance so much? Or is it just the adorable way he adds 'Daddy' to the end of his bratty rebuttal that gets me deep in my core?

Or maybe it's that he's still sitting on your cock like a good boy...

My inner thoughts might be onto something.

"Well, baby," I respond with exaggerated patience, feeding

him an olive and a cube of cheese, held together by a toothpick, "when you're with me, I'm going to make sure that you're fed properly."

"I do like it when you feed me," he agrees. "When I'm Big or Little."

I think he just likes being looked after. I get the feeling he hasn't had a lot of that in his life. Instead of voicing my suspicions, though, I smile. "I've told you before: I love taking care of you no matter your headspace."

He's quiet for a long moment after that, buying himself some time to reply by sipping at his wine again. I sip at mine, too, listening to the quiet soundtrack of Christmas carols playing out of the small speaker near the tree. They're mostly instrumentals, chosen because they made me think of the snow globe at the cabin. The one which Anson adored.

"This should all feel too fast," he eventually muses out loud, leaning back against me. He rests his head on my shoulder, nuzzling his forehead against the underside of my jaw. "It doesn't," he continues, "but it should."

"Who makes the rules on how we should feel?" I can't help but counter. "Who says how fast feelings should develop? And why do we have to listen to them anyway?"

"That sounds incredibly idealistic for a man who, only a couple of weeks ago, was a grumpy hermit-type wanting to avoid any and all festivity or cheer."

Rolling my eyes, I resist the urge to tickle his bare sides. "So sue me, I had a change of heart. That can happen, you know." My tone softens out into something warmer and more affectionate, and I turn my head to kiss his forehead. "You made me feel again, baby. I know that sounds cheesy, but…being your Daddy over Christmas was…well, it was magical. It was more than just playing a part for a scene or scratching an itch. I got to see you exploring your Little side for the first time and that…that was something really special, sunshine." Tears spring to my eyes as unexpected emotion swoops through me. "You really did brighten my world again."

Just when I think I've been too sappy, Anson sniffles. "I love you so much, Daddy."

"And I love you." I kiss his temple softly. "Merry Christmas, baby." Then, glancing at the clock on the wall, I add, "And Happy New Year, too."

Chapter Twenty-Three - Anson

Being seated on Daddy's cock is awesome, but it's starting to make me very horny. Feeding each other isn't helping that feeling to fade, either. But, at the same time as I feel the urge to bounce a little, I want to just enjoy this connection between us.

When Daddy softly wishes me a Happy New Year, it registers that we just ended last year and started this one literally joined together. That makes me really happy. It's probably the most blatant metaphor ever, but I love it. We're connected now, hopefully for the foreseeable future.

"I know it's not Christmas anymore, but would you like to open your presents?" Daddy asks after I spend a moment too long basking in being so close to him that he's actually inside me.

I'm hovering in this strange headspace where I'm neither Big or Little. Sucking my lower lip for a moment, I ask, "Should I be Little for that?"

"Whatever you want, sunshine," his big, warm, callused hand

rubs my hip. It makes me squirm a little, and we both groan when the movement stimulates his cock inside me, making it bump against my prostate. "There are gifts with both your headspaces in mind."

"You're spoiling me," I tell him, unable to prevent grinning a little wickedly. "It's almost like you *want* me to be a brat."

"I do want to spank that perfect ass of yours," he admits with a chuckle, nuzzling his beard into the crook of my neck, "but I really did just want to give you the Christmas you deserved for your first time as a Little." He pauses, then seems to correct himself, "For anytime, really."

"I *knew* you were a big teddy bear under that gruff lumber-snack exterior."

He groans, but I can hear the affection in the sound. It sends a thrill up my spine because *he loves me*. When I first realized what I'd said back at the hospital, I had prepared a whole speech about saying it by accident, like a trained response, and I had hoped that he'd buy the excuse and not let my accidental confession make things weird between us. That had been my best-case scenario.

But then he said it back, and he did all of this sweet stuff for me, and he blew my best-case scenario right out of the water, replacing it with something even better.

"In all seriousness, though," I tell him before he can protest my description, "thank you. Really. This" —I gesture around the room— "is the sweetest thing anyone has ever done for me. It's a bit overwhelming. But in a good way!" I hurry to add.

The hair of his beard brushes the back of my shoulder before his lips meet my skin. "I'm glad you like it."

Glancing back over to the immaculately decorated tree and the pile of gifts underneath it, I bite my lip again. "I think I'd like to open my Big presents first, if that's okay? Then maybe I can be Little for the rest of the night?"

"You never have to ask permission to regress, honey. I love you Little or Big or anywhere in between."

Drake groans again as I try to turn in his lap, and I ignore the momentary discomfort I cause myself by reflexively clenching around him. "I really lucked out with you, didn't I?"

"That feeling is mutual, Anson. I hope you realize that."

"I do," I assure him, because he has made his feelings more than obvious. I appreciate that more than he can possibly know. But instead of saying any of that, I carefully move our wine and food out of the way, and then I start to bounce in his lap.

Breath hitching, his hands grip my hips. "Fuck, baby…"

I don't love that I can't see his face, but when I lean my head back onto his shoulder and he starts to thrust up into me, I can feel his ecstasy and enjoyment. It's in his shallow breaths, and in the way his hands sweep over my abdomen and down to my cock. It's in the messy kisses he presses to my temple and the side of my mouth.

I don't even realize I'm making desperate "oh…oh…oh" sounds with every little bounce on his cock until he tells me how much he loves it.

"I need it harder," I demand, still surprising myself that I enjoy taking his cock at all. How have I gone so long without knowing how good this can feel? Or, maybe, it was that I just hadn't met the right person to make it feel good.

He stops moving —the complete opposite of what I was asking for— and his big palm pushes at the middle of my back. "Hands and knees, baby. On three."

Counting down, we make it happen, moving together while

maintaining our connection. It's as though we silently agreed that it would suck to separate, even for a few seconds.

"This okay?" Drake pants as he starts to move, taking advantage of the change in position. His thrusts become longer and deeper, making me moan.

"Yes, Daddy. Harder."

With his fingertips digging into my hips, he complies. It is absolutely perfect. Communication devolves into a series of grunts and groans and whimpers. My "oh, oh, oh"s escalate into sharp cries of "yes, yes, yes" and "there, right there"s.

"Fuck, baby, I love how vocal you are," Drake praises between heavy breaths. "Tell Daddy what you like. What you need."

"M-my cock. Jerk my—oh, God, yes!" I've leaked so much precum that the glide of his hand over my shaft is effortless. "Oh, God, Daddy…I'm going to come."

"Do it," he encourages, sounding strained and breathless. I shut my eyes as his hand squeezes just a bit tighter around my cock, stroking me faster. "Come for me. Be my good boy. Come for Daddy."

That's all it takes to send me hurtling over the edge. "Fuck, Daddy! Fuck, fuck, *fuuuuuck!*"

I barely register his answering, gravelly "fuck, baby" as my orgasm triggers his, because I'm too busy collapsing from how surprisingly intense my own was. My heart is hammering wildly and my head is spinning.

Definitely a very happy New Year to me!

* * *

"Daddy! It's a doctor's bag!" I hold up the gift I've just unwrapped; a child's play pretend medical kit, complete with plastic stethoscope, thermometer, blood pressure cuff and reflex hammer, among other things. I've already opened a variety of other presents, including some new Little clothes, toy cars, and stuffies, but this one has got me super excited. "Daddy, the box says the stethoscope works!"

"It does," Daddy replies indulgently, and his smile makes me feel all gooey inside.

In the end, we went to bed after we had sex last night, and when I woke up I wanted to be Little, which meant I got *extremely* animated about the gifts under the Christmas tree. I haven't looked at any of my Big headspace presents, but I don't think Daddy minds that. They'll be there when I'm ready to be Big again.

I can feel a sly grin quirking my lips when I ask, "Can we play doctor, Daddy?"

"You're insatiable, aren't you?" He chuckles.

"I don't know what that big word means." Relishing in his amused snort, I hold up my gift again, making my eyes as round and pleading as I can. "Please, Daddy?"

"You know I can't resist you when you ask so nicely."

I scramble to open up my toy medical bag, pulling all the bits and pieces out of their packaging and then putting them all into the old-school style bag. Then I remember my coat. I brought one with me after my shift last night!

Clamoring to my feet, I snatch up my bag and tell Daddy to stay in the waiting room until I call him in for his exam. His renewed chuckles follow me down the hallway to his bedroom.

Once I'm there, I strip all the way out of my onesie and diaper, putting on my white coat and nothing else. Kicking my pile of discarded clothes out of the way, I head back into the makeshift waiting room.

I make a show of pretending to look around the room at my many waiting patients, then ask, "Mister Daddy?" as though the name could belong to anyone there.

He nods and pushes to his feet, and the look on his face is stuck somewhere between amused and horny.

"This way, please," I tell him, turning around and leading the way to my pretend consulting room. Once we're there, I point at the bed. "Take a seat." He does as told. I reach for my medical bag and hang the stethoscope around my neck. "Now, Mister Daddy, what brings you here today?"

"Just a general checkup," he answers easily. "I have to make sure I'm in good shape so I can look after my Boy at home, you see."

I nod. "Yes, that is important." I hum as I look him over, now feeling a spark of impatience. "You should take off all your clothes now."

Daddy startles and laughs. "Buy me a drink first, Doc."

I giggle, then remember that I'm the doctor and try to put my serious face back on. Raising my chin, I explain, "I need to give you a thor…thur…um…*in-depth* exam, Daddy."

"If you say so, Doc."

Though his words are teasing, he does what I asked, taking off his shirt, sweatpants, and underwear.

I grin at his erection and he arches an eyebrow before glancing down at my hardening cock.

It takes all my willpower to keep playing the game, listening to his heart and breathing through the plastic stethoscope, tapping his knee with the plastic reflex hammer, and then taking his temperature orally with the pretend thermometer.

"It all looks pretty good," I tell him, "but now I think you need a full physical, too."

"Oh? Isn't that what you were doing?"

Shaking my head, I set my toys aside and run my hands over his hairy chest, massaging his muscles as I take my time exploring him. When I get to his straining cock, I take myself in hand as well.

Daddy smacks my forearm —the one attached to the hand on my own erection— and *'tsk'*s. "This is my exam, Doctor. You shouldn't be touching yourself."

I whine. "But Daddy—"

"Nope. Let your cock go, sunshine."

"Will you touch me, Daddy?"

He shakes his head. "You're the doctor here. I'm the patient."

I pout exaggeratedly. *"Please*, Daddy?"

"You know, I don't even think a doctor should be touching my cock, either..."

I gasp. "But—"

"Keep going with my exam, please, Doctor Anson." There's a challenging glint in his eyes and I realize that he wants me to break the new rules.

As much as he's threatened to spank me, I haven't yet given him a reason to.

This is my chance to be a little bratty.

Understanding my new mission, I pretend to do as he has said, getting out the blood pressure cuff and wrapping it around his big, brawny bicep. When I play with the squeezy air-pump, I casually trail my free hand back down his body and then stroke his cock again.

"Anson..." he says in warning.

"Oops?" I reply, unable to hide my smile, but I do remove my hand again.

"This is your first and only warning," he tells me. "If you

disobey me again, you will be going over my lap."

I can't hide the way my cock jumps happily at the threat. Who would have thought the idea of being spanked would ever appeal to me?

A lot of the appeal is in getting to try something new with Daddy, I think. But I can't deny that I feel a thrill at disobeying him, too. A feeling of excitement at being naughty and risking the consequences in a controlled environment. It's like a micro-adrenaline rush, knowing that I'm controlling the situation, that I get to decide when my punishment will be delivered.

There's a tickle of anticipation and almost-fear there, too, because I know that Daddy's palm on my bare ass is going to sting and maybe even mark me up.

But I do want it.

We return to playing, and I pull out a plastic syringe and pretend to give him a shot, then offer to kiss his boo-boo better. He lets me do that and, the moment my lips meet his skin, I can't resist reaching for his dick again, my heart thumping wildly at this deliberate act of defiance.

"That's it," he growls, grabbing my wrist, "you were warned, baby."

He's got me bent over his lap in a blink, and cool air breezes over my ass as my coat is lifted and folded over my back. I shiver, whether at the cool air or anticipation, I'm not completely sure.

"Good boys listen to their Daddy, Anson," he says, and his hand rubs over my left cheek in firm circles. "Did you listen to me?" His hand shifts to my right cheek and repeats the motion. I shiver again.

"N-no, Daddy."

"You're going to get ten smacks for disobeying me," he says.

Then, gently he asks, "Do you remember your safe words?"

"Red light to stop," I answer, feeling a bit jittery now.

"Good. If it's too much, or you hate this, you use that safe word."

The jittery feeling eases a bit, knowing that I'm still in control here. This is for fun. It's going to hurt, but I can stop if it's not something my Little side needs after all.

With how hard my cock is and how fast my heart is beating, I don't think I'm going to hate it, though.

"Yes, Daddy."

"There's my good boy," he croons, then follows it with, "I want you to count the spanks, okay?"

"Yes, Daddy."

"God, the things you do to me…" he mutters under his breath. I'm proud of myself for half a second, before a stinging, resounding *smack* lands on my ass and I jolt forward with the shock of it.

"W…One," I remember to count, hearing the breathlessness of my own voice.

His palm meets my flesh twice more in rapid succession, making me gasp and wince. "Two, three."

"Good boy," he praises, and I feel him rubbing my skin soothingly. The praise fills me with warmth, even though I know there's more to come.

By the time we've reached seven, my lip is quivering, but I can't explain why. It's not like the pain is unbearable. In fact, I think he's going easy on me. But I feel like I'm getting more and more Little, even while my dick is getting harder with how surprisingly hot this whole situation is.

Tears trickle down my cheeks at "N-nine", and I cry out "Ten!" when Daddy lands his final smack, but I'm oblivious to that. My head feels super floaty, like I've just had the most intense orgasm of my life and I'm drifting in the afterglow.

I could get used to this.

Chapter Twenty-Four – Drake

I am about ninety-eight percent sure that Anson just found subspace. This is kind of a mindfuck for me because I've never had a Boy get there before, and certainly not during our first experiment with a spanking scene. But he's gone quiet and limp, with his cum dribbling down the side of my thigh, and he's either in subspace or I've broken him.

It's gotta be the former, right?

God, I hope so.

When he suggested playing doctor this morning, I naïvely assumed he wanted to play with his new toys in Littlespace. I didn't think he meant *playing doctor.* And, obviously, what followed was a super cute and sexy hybrid of both fantasies. I loved every minute of that, and finally getting to spank his irresistible ass was the cherry on top.

And now that he's flying high on the endorphin rush, I'm glad that we did.

I move us until we're lying down on the bed, holding him in my arms, relishing the intimacy of the moment. I'm not going to rush him to come out of his current headspace, and I'm content to cuddle him until he does.

He's not asleep, but his eyes are glazed and droopy, and the little smile tugging at the corners of his lips reassures me that he's okay. I kiss his forehead and snuggle against him, breathing in the scent of his slightly-sweaty hair.

Not for the first time in the past week, I marvel at how right he feels in my arms. It's hard to believe that it has only been a week, to be honest. For how strongly I love him, and for how well we click together, you'd be forgiven for assuming we've known each other for months, or even years.

I can't imagine a future without him here with me anymore.

It's too soon to ask him to move in with me, but it won't be long before my resolve breaks and I do. I've spent too much time on my own, depriving myself of the joys of being a Daddy for more than the occasional scene at The Grove, to not give myself the happy ending I so desperately want, especially when Anson has already hinted that he wants the same things that I do.

He doesn't want to be Little all the time, but he's happy for me to be Daddy all the time. He hates being lonely, and so do I. We love each other and work well together. There's no reason for me to hold back for too long, except out of a sense of propriety.

And who sets those rules anyway? Who says how long we should date before it's socially acceptable for us to move in together? And who the fuck cares what those people think anyway?

Anson stretches and makes a cute sound at the back of his throat, cutting off my train of thought. I'll revisit the idea of eventually asking him to move in later. For now, I have a Boy to take care of.

And I'm going to enjoy every minute of it.

Inviting my crush to my cabin for Christmas might just have been the best decision I have ever made, and I can't wait to see what the future holds for us.

Epilogue – Anson

"They're here!" I cry in excitement as I hear car doors slamming shut outside. "Daddy, hurry!" I race to the front door from the living room, my socked feet slipping and skidding on the tiled floor.

"What have I told you about running in the house?" Daddy admonishes with exasperation. "You're going to hurt yourself one of these days."

"Nuh-uh," I argue, "I'm a doctor. I'll be fine."

"That's what you said when you refused to let me change you the other week," he replies calmly. "And what happened then?"

I scrunch my nose with annoyance. "I was playin' with my train." And there's something about staying in my diaper after I've wet it that makes me feel even littler than normal. I'd wanted to hold onto that feeling.

"What happened, Anson?"

Sighing, I mumble, "I got a rash." Before he can act all superior about it, I add, "But only a tiny one. Barely an irta…

irra…itter…*ugh.* Barely *anything.*"

"I was still right, though, wasn't I?"

He's *still* not making any attempt to open the door.

"*Daddy,*" I whine, "they're here!"

"You know," he folds his arms and stares me down, the stern look making my tummy go all bubbly while my dick starts to wake up, "if you're going to be like this today, maybe I'll cancel the playdate and give you corner time instead."

Daddy has discovered the one actual punishment I truly hate, and he knows it.

Corner time.

Blergh.

It's so *boring* in the corner. I'm not allowed to talk, or dance, or sing, or color, or play with my toys…it's stupid and I hate it.

"No!" I plead. "I'll be good, I promise!"

Daddy smirks and shakes his head, finally moving towards the door. "I love you, sunshine, but we all know how impulsive you can be when you're excited. Don't go making promises you can't keep."

I know he's just teasing me, so I poke my tongue out at him. I declare, "You're so mean, Daddy," right as he opens the door.

"It sounds like someone is halfway to a spanking already," Vince laughs, his hand in the air as though he was poised to knock. "Which really doesn't surprise me." He shifts his hand and knocks it against Daddy's fist. "Hey, man, thanks for the invite."

"Anytime." Daddy chuckles and steps aside to let Vinnie in, and I ignore my best friend in preference of throwing my arms around his boyfriend instead.

"Hey, Bear! Your Daddy's a meanie, too." I tell him in a stage whisper. "Let's go play and let them be mean and boring on their own."

Bear grins at me, the freckled skin over his cheeks and nose stretching with the wide smile. He shakes his head and his mop of red curls flies around his face. "My Daddy isn't mean. You're just being naughty."

That makes me gasp and clutch at my chest. "I am not! I'm a good boy!"

All three of them laugh at me. I pout. "Well, fu—er—fluff you all."

"Oh, it's started already, huh?" Charlie's voice, full of amusement, asks from the doorway. He looks over at me and smirks. "You've been hanging out with my brother again, haven't you?"

Ash pushes past his Daddy to wrap me in a hug. "There's nothing wrong with being playful," he tells me. "Also, Merry Christmas, Anson."

I hug him back, too excited and happy to keep up the pretense of being annoyed with any of them. "Merry Christmas!"

Over the past year, these guys have become my closest friends. We've had playdates and cookouts together, gone to The Grove and also hung out without the role play, too. (Well, except for Bear, who is pretty much always Little, but we love him that way.) They've been there for me as I've explored every facet of age play that I could possibly think of, working out what I enjoy and what I'd rather avoid.

Daddy's also become more social, at least with Vinnie and Charlie and some of the others from The Grove, and our dynamic has only become better for it. Back in those early months, he confessed that he felt out of practice with being a full-time Daddy, so I think it has helped him to have other Daddies to talk to and get advice from.

He's gotten particularly close with Vince, which makes me happy considering they're my two favorite people in the whole wide world, but it sucks when they both team up over my more frustrating qualities. But that's where Ash and Bear come in for me. They're my fellow Littles and, even though Bear is a bit of a Daddy's boy and goodie-two-shoes, they still encourage me to be as silly and Little as I want to be, even when it makes Daddy and Vince sigh with exasperation.

Let's be real, though: that exasperation is totally just an act on Daddy's part. He loves me having fun…and I know that he loves coming up with sexy punishments for me, too. And that's what I'm pushing for today. I want Daddy to tie me to the headboard and edge me until I'm in tears, so I'm being just a little bit sassier and naughtier than usual.

It's one of the silent games Daddy and I play.

The past year really has changed everything for me. I've gone from not knowing where I fit in in the kink lifestyle, to being comfortable and happy almost all the time. I've gone from feeling lonely to having someone to come home to every day. I've gone from living in a tiny, personality-free apartment to a real home with my Daddy.

Oh, and probably the biggest life changer: I've gone from stressing out all the time to knowing that I can just let go and be free once I'm home. Adult problems aren't really a problem for me anymore because Daddy takes care of them. I transfer him money to pay for the utilities and stuff, but he deals with managing it all for me. The only time I have to spend worrying about Big issues is when I'm at work, and even that seems easier to handle with everything else taken care of.

It still feels surreal at times.

A year ago, I was driving to Daddy's cabin thinking I was

just going to hide away from everyone else's happiness over Christmas. I never once thought I would find my own there. Sometimes, I even think that maybe I crashed my car badly and I've been in a coma, fantasizing the life I've been living for the past year. It seems too fantastic and too easy to be real. But then Daddy will cuddle me close and assure me that it is real, that I'm giving him a Happily Ever After that he never imagined that he could have, too, and that makes those thoughts go away.

Somehow, we found each other last Christmas. So, this Christmas and for every Christmas from now on, we plan on celebrating that fact with our closest friends —people we agree played a pretty big part in us getting together and staying together. Without their support and advice over the past year, things might have turned out differently. Or they might not have. Daddy and I *are* very good at communicating, after all.

Which takes me back to the silent communication we've become experts at. I wink at him before I drag Ash and Bear into the living room to indulge our Little sides in front of the Christmas tree Daddy and I decorated together on December First (yet another ritual we're starting, because he says it's something we both deserve to enjoy properly, though I will always cherish that low-budget, impromptu Christmas in his cabin).

Daddy winks back at me.

I'm so *getting my sexy punishment tonight!*

It's going to be a very Merry Christmas indeed.

The End

* * *

Thank you so much for reading *Anson's Awakening*. I genuinely hope you liked it as much as I enjoyed writing it. I set out to write a ridiculously sweet Christmas age play romance and I think I succeeded, haha.

Anyway, I'd love it if you could leave a review on your retailer of choice or on Goodreads or StoryGraph. Reviews not only tell the algorithms that our books deserve attention, but honest feedback also encourages and inspires me to keep writing. Even a star rating helps, and I greatly appreciate you making time to do so.

Speaking of my writing: if you'd like a free ebook copy of *Charlie's Contentment* (a 10,000 word zero-angst, high-fluff novella following Asher & Charlie on their honeymoon) subscribe to my newsletter here:

https://annasparrows.com/newsletter-subscription/

For updates, release dates, competitions and more, follow me on Facebook. The link is in the 'About The Author' page.

DKAG Christmas Daddies

This multi author series features books with Daddies, boys/littles, age gap, age play, and more. Your favorite authors are bringing all the holiday romance vibes with stories sure to warm your heart. They can be read in any order as each title is unique to the author's world. Be sure to grab them all!

December 1st

His Temporary Assistant by A.W. Scott

December 6th

Daddy Santa's Snow Angel by Aria Grace

December 10th

Anson's Awakening by Anna Sparrows

December 13th

Satan's Little Helpers by Athena Steller

December 17th
Daddy's Little Drummer Boy by Della Cain

December 20th
In Good Spirits by Helen Juliet

December 23rd
Our Little Sebastian by Myf Wren

December 31st
A Little Cinny Latte by Kota Quinn

About the Author

I've been writing for as long as I can remember. I started with silly short stories as a kid, moved on to fanfiction in my teens, and began publishing my own romance novels in my thirties.

I've read MM romances of all sub-genres for decades (ask me about my love of Spander fanfic, haha), and I finally wrote my own sweet & kinky MM romance in 2022. The reader response to that changed my life.

And thus, Anna Sparrows was born.

When I'm not writing, I'm exploring South East Queensland with my partner, our kids, and our dog.

*All of my writing is 100% my own. No part of it is generated by Artificial Intelligence (AI) software of any kind. Yes, that means that it's sometimes flawed, but I'm okay with that.

You can connect with me on:
- https://annasparrows.com
- https://www.facebook.com/AnnaSparrowsAuthor
- https://www.instagram.com/annasparrows

Subscribe to my newsletter:
- https://annasparrows.com/newsletter-subscription

Also by Anna Sparrows

I write ridiculously sweet & steamy MM romance with guaranteed HEAs…and sometimes with a side of kink. My backlist can be found at annasparrows.com

Littles & Lace Series
The Littles & Lace series is an MM Age Play series, following a group of like-minded friends in the BDSM community. You'll find mild ABDL, light Pet Play, Femme Play and more here.

Book 1: Asher's Answer

Book 2: Matteo's Mettle

Book 3: Ted's Temerity

Book 4: Spencer's Satisfaction

Book 5: Chance's Choice

Book 6: Josh's Jackpot

Dads & Adages Series
Visit Australia's sunny Gold Coast where an assortment of single dads find love and even learn a few life lessons along the way.

Book 1: Where There's A Will

Book 2: You Don't Know Jack

Book 3: A Match Made In Evan (release TBA)

Shifters Sanctuary Series
In a world where alphas are thought to be extinct, a number of men are about to have their worlds rocked.

Book 1: His Alpha Unlocked

Book 2: His Prodigal Alpha

Book 3: His Unicorn Alpha (release TBA)

A Surprise For The Holidays
Written in 3rd person POV, *A Surprise for the Holidays* is a sweet, fluffy MM Christmas novella with a grumpy former soccer player turned coach, a golden retriever younger player, and a precocious little girl. Featuring an Aussie Christmas, grumpy/sunshine vibes, an age gap and sand where you're used to snow, this novella brings additional heat to the festive season in more ways than one!

Down Under Daddies Series
Set in rural Western Australia, come meet the and the kinkiest and queerest band of stationhands any outback cattle station has ever seen.

Book 1: A Stable Daddy